'A Robinson Crusoe-esque story of a summer
of survival in a modern setting but with primitive
resources. It is rivetingly and entertainingly
told, with heart and tension.'
Sunday Times, Children's Book of the Week

'Enthralling and uplifting, this story of survival and
belonging is perfect for adventure lovers of 9+.'
The Guardian

'Unsworth's book is tense and vivid, her band of misfits
proving that the weak can win out and that wherever you
go can be a paradise if you want it to be.'
Literary Review

'A powerful message underpins this gripping
and contemporary drama.'
Daily Mail

'Strong, engaging, and powerful story about hope and
survival. Completely engaging, it will keep
you enthralled until the very end.'
School Librarian

'A sublime tale of trust, survival, friendship
and human connection.'
LoveReading4Kids

'A tense and atmospheric adventure.'
CLPE

'Here's a book I'd love to use as a class reader
or read aloud but I'll also be recommending it
highly as a "read for pleasure". Buy it and try it! 5*.'
ReadingZone

The Time Traveller and the TIGER

'A winning time-slip tale...'
Sunday Times, Children's Book of the Week

'Environmental, racial and social concerns are deftly woven into a gloriously warm, heart-stopping adventure...'
New Statesman

'A beautifully written and thought-provoking mix of adventure, time travel and historical story with strong, engaging characters and themes of friendship, righting wrongs, and conservation...'
Books for Keeps

The Girl who thought her Mother was a Mermaid

'The story is teasing and suspenseful, and written with vivacity and elegance.'
Sunday Times, Children's Book of the Week

'Tania Unsworth writes beautifully, and it's hard not to get caught in the current of this magical tale about family and identity.'
The Times

'Lyrical writing with a hint of dark magic in a tale of grief, loss and finding yourself.'
The Bookseller

NOWHERE ISLAND

NOWHERE ISLAND

TANIA UNSWORTH

ZEPHYR

An imprint of Head of Zeus

This is a Zephyr book first published in the UK in 2023
by Head of Zeus, part of Bloomsbury Publishing Plc

This paperback edition first published in 2024 by Head of Zeus,
part of Bloomsbury Publishing Plc

9 7 5 3 1 2 4 6 8

A catalogue record for this book is available from the British Library.

ISBN (PB): 9781804540091
ISBN (E): 9781804540060

Cover design by Kimberley Walker
Typeset by Ed Pickford

Printed and bound in Great Britain by
CPI Group (UK) Ltd, Croydon CR0 4YY

Head of Zeus
5–8 Hardwick Street
London EC1R 4RG

WWW.HEADOFZEUS.COM

For Steph Richardson and Una Flood.
Thank you for the days…

One

Gil escaped just after his twelfth birthday, in the middle of the afternoon. He did it on impulse, although he must have been thinking about it for a while, because he picked the perfect car – an SUV with a single driver and plenty of space in the back. He also picked the perfect time.

They were at a petrol station. Ms Lundy was filling the tank and staring at her phone at the same time. The SUV was six metres away, on the other side of the row of pumps. The driver had got out and was rummaging through her bag for a credit card.

Gil couldn't explain what happened next. It was as if his mind had switched off and left his body to do all the thinking. He grabbed his backpack and silently opened the door of Ms Lundy's car. Then he slipped out and dropped to the ground, crouching as he pushed the door almost – but not quite – shut. Seconds later, he was in the back seat of the SUV. He took a deep breath and lifted his head.

Ms Lundy hadn't moved. The driver of the SUV had finally found her credit card and was peering at the pump, tapping buttons. Gil took the opportunity to scramble into the far back. It was empty apart from a suitcase and a blanket. He crawled into the gap between the suitcase and the seat back, covered himself with the blanket and lay still.

Gil knew Ms Lundy wouldn't immediately return to the car after filling the tank because she'd said she was going to get a coffee from the station store. That would give him a little time.

He listened to the gurgling sound of petrol pouring into the SUV, wondering how long it would take to fill. Perhaps, if he was lucky, the driver would be one of those nervous people who topped up the tank when it was only half-empty.

Or perhaps – if he was even more lucky – the station store would be busy, and Ms Lundy would have to wait to get her coffee. Gil imagined a queue of customers. There were three – no, four – people. The man at the front was buying engine oil, only he couldn't make up his mind which brand. He was heavyset, sweating as he hitched up the waist of his baggy cargo shorts…

Gil spent a lot of time making up stories. Not because he thought it could make them come true, but because – for a few moments – it made them *feel* true. And those were the only moments in his life when he ever felt completely certain of anything.

He concentrated. There was an old woman in the queue, he decided, and a teenager carrying a little kid who was trying to grab sweets from the display. Ms Lundy was standing at the end, wearing her 'I-have-all-the-time-in-the-world' face, and secretly glancing at her watch every few seconds.

The stream of petrol cut off, and footsteps came around the side of the SUV. The door opened and the driver heaved a sigh as she settled into her seat.

Start the engine! Gil shouted in his head.

He heard muttering and a rustling sound. As if the driver was searching through her bag, wondering if she'd forgotten anything.

You haven't, you haven't, Gil begged, feeling the start of panic. What if the station store hadn't been busy? What if Ms Lundy had gone to the counter, paid for her coffee, and come straight out? She might be walking back to her car right that minute. Raising her hand against the sun, squinting through the windscreen at the empty passenger seat.

'Go! Go! Go!' he whispered in despair.

As if in answer, he heard the soft roar of the ignition. They were moving. Gil felt the SUV make a wide turn of the petrol station on to the exit ramp, the hum of the motorway growing louder and louder. The driver paused, waiting for a break in the traffic, then accelerated to join the flow.

It was too late to turn back. Gil was engulfed by terror. He'd chosen the SUV at random. Ms Lundy would have no idea where he'd gone. And every passing minute was carrying him another mile away. He lifted a corner of the blanket and looked through the rear window. The sky was completely clear, apart from a cloud, drifting far and free across the blue. At the sight of it, Gil's fear vanished and a surge of exhilaration took its place.

Other people had always decided where he should go. He'd spent his whole life being taken to one place after another. Now, for the first time ever, he wasn't being taken anywhere.

He was going all by himself.

If he'd been able to, Gil would have cheered out loud. Instead, he reached into his backpack and retrieved a dark, yellow pebble.

It was ordinary looking, no different from a million others, except that the ocean had drilled a dime-sized hole right through the middle. Looking through the hole made a strange thing happen. Everything looked much nearer. And at the same time, everything looked much further away.

Gil raised the pebble to his eye and stared at the sky until his heart settled and his breath grew calm.

Two

It was deliciously cool in the SUV, even under the blanket. Gil almost fell asleep listening to the soft drone of the air conditioning.

In twenty miles take exit fifteen on the right, towards route eighty-two east.

'Okay, okay,' the driver said in a loud voice. 'You told me that already.'

Gil heard a rustle of plastic. 'I might as well have that sandwich,' she announced in the same loud voice. 'Half of it, anyway…'

She must be lonely, Gil thought, *talking to herself like that*. Or maybe she just liked to imagine she had someone real to chat to, for the same reason Gil liked to imagine things. To make the world seem okay.

He wondered what Ms Lundy had done when she'd found him gone. At first, she'd think he was in the bathroom, or stretching his legs. She would have waited for a few minutes, then gone to look. But the petrol station was small. It wouldn't have taken Ms Lundy long to realise he wasn't there and call for the police.

Poor Ms Lundy. Gil hoped she wouldn't get in trouble. She'd always been kind to him. He knew this didn't mean much, because it was her job to be kind to him, but he appreciated the effort she made.

'I know you're going to be happy in the new place,' she'd said as they set out that morning. 'I'm sure it will be fine this time.'

Gil could have pointed out that she'd said the same thing about the last place she'd taken him. But he didn't.

He was much too kind himself, to say something like that.

Gil was five years old when his parents were drowned in a kayaking accident. Nobody could explain how it happened. The weather that day was warm and clear, without a breath of wind, and the sea shone like a mirror. As Gil's mother and father set off across the bay, there was nothing to break their reflection but the dip of their own paddles. Yet they were never seen again. One minute they were there – two dots on the bright horizon – next minute they were gone.

Gil could remember bits and pieces of his life before the accident. But his memories were so few, and he had gone over them so many times, that they'd grown thin, like a coat patched and patched again, until almost nothing of the original was left. All he knew for sure was that his parents had loved him with all their hearts.

He was an only child, and his mum and dad were only children too, so Gil had no relatives to look after him when his parents died. Instead, Ms Lundy was put in charge of his case. She was a social worker, and the first thing she did was send him to a temporary foster home.

Gil didn't remember much about the foster home, except that he was given an orange teddy bear with eyes like two fried eggs. Gil had a feeling he was supposed to love the bear, but he didn't. No matter where he went, its enormous eyes seemed to follow him. He tried stuffing the bear under the bed, but he could still feel it staring. Through the bedsprings and the mattress, all the way up to where he lay, alone in the strange-shaped dark.

When Ms Lundy came to pick him up, Gil tried to leave the teddy behind, but the lady who'd been fostering him ran out of the house at the last minute.

'You forgot your toy!' she said, thrusting it into his arms.

The teddy sat on Gil's lap, staring at him as they drove away.

'That's a cute bear,' Ms Lundy said.

'I hate it,' Gil cried. And before Ms Lundy could stop him, he rolled down the window and threw the bear from the car. It hit the black top in a blur of orange fur, bounced and vanished from sight.

The instant it was gone, Gil felt terrible. He pictured the bear lying on the side of the road, ugly and unwanted, with no one for company but the wind in the grass.

It's okay, he told himself as they sped away. *Someone will find it. A girl with weird, too-big eyes will pick it up and love it because it looks just like her.*

Even at five years old, Gil was good at making up stories.

Over the next few years, he was sent to foster home after foster home, always hoping that he would be adopted. Somehow, it never happened. One couple discovered they were having twins and couldn't look after Gil as well. Another had to change their plans because of illness and a third failed to meet the strict rules of adoption. As Gil got older, the search became even more difficult, because most people were looking for a younger child to take care of. Not a boy who'd be a teenager in a year or two.

By the time he was twelve, Gil had lost count of the number of homes he'd stayed in. And despite Ms Lundy's cheerful promises, he had also lost hope.

He was tired of being shuffled from place to place, never knowing how long he would stay, or where he'd go next. He was tired of always having to be on his best behaviour. Most of all, he was tired of telling himself the same story; the story of how – one day – he would find a family where love wasn't doled out like pocket money, to be taken away when you did something wrong. Somehow or other (the precise details were always changing) Gil would become part of this family. Not because he was good, or clever, or tidy or polite or got on well with others or it happened to be convenient, but because that was just the way it was.

The story had comforted Gil when he was small, but it didn't any longer. In fact, it made things worse, because the gap between the story and reality seemed to widen with each new place he went.

As he sat waiting for Ms Lundy to fill the tank before taking him to yet another stranger's home, with a history he would never learn and a collection of family photographs to which his would never be added, all Gil knew for sure was that he couldn't go through it again. Anything would be better than that.

Even getting into a random car, with no idea where it was going, or what he would do when it arrived.

Three

Gil found half a packet of mints in the pocket of his jeans. He ate them slowly, watching as evening turned the sky a watery pink. The car radio was on. He could hear piano music, the notes falling sad and sweet as the miles rolled by. He closed his eyes and slept.

It was pitch dark when he woke. He could see nothing but the dazzle of headlights as cars approached from behind, blinding him for a second before they overtook. His body ached all over, and he was so thirsty that he was almost tempted to give himself up and beg the driver for something to drink. But she might crash the car from surprise. And even if she didn't, he would still be sent back.

Ms Lundy wouldn't shout at him, or tell him off. Instead, she'd be kinder than ever. Somehow that would feel much worse.

I would rather die of thirst, Gil thought.

If the driver of the SUV had been travelling any faster, she might never have spotted the shape on the side of the motorway. She was nervous about driving in the dark though and ever since nightfall, she had kept to the slow lane, her eyes wide as she concentrated on the road.

For a second it was there, clear in her headlights. Then it was gone.

'What was that?' she said out loud. 'Was that a *dog*?'

Gil felt the SUV veer. They were turning into a rest area of some kind. They pulled up, the engine still running and the headlights on.

'Oh my goodness!' the driver cried.

Gil let go of his backpack and raised his head, holding his breath as he peered over the back of the seat.

The dog was thin, with long legs and a snout so sharp it looked as if it had been whittled to a point by a knife. As Gil watched, it took a few limping steps, then stopped and looked back.

'Oh my goodness,' the driver repeated. She got out of the SUV, leaving the door open. 'What are you doing here?'

The dog stared at her and twitched its tail. Encouraged, she dropped to her heels. Her fingers grazed the top of the dog's head. Then it backed away, just out of reach.

Gil ducked abruptly. The driver was coming back. She rummaged about on the front seat, muttering to herself. He waited until she had gone back to the dog before lifting his head.

The driver was holding something. Gil guessed it was the other half of her sandwich. She tore off a scrap and tossed it to the dog. He was on it in a flash, moving with a ravenous speed that would have been alarming if it hadn't been so pitiful.

'Why, you're *starving*,' she said, tearing off another scrap and offering it to the dog.

Gil had a feeling they might be there for some time. He could tell the driver wouldn't leave until she'd given the stray all the food she could find. She probably wouldn't be able to catch him – he looked far too wild for that. But what if she *did* manage to get him into the SUV? With a nose that sharp, the dog would sniff him out in an instant. There was no way he could stay hidden…

He was so intent on watching what happened next, that he barely heard a soft *click* behind him. It wasn't until he felt a breeze on the back of his neck that he turned. The rear door of the SUV was part-open. As he stared, too shocked to move or make a sound, he saw an arm reach through the gap, fingers groping.

'Hey!' Gil said, finally finding his voice. 'What are you *doing*?'

It was too late. The arm had vanished.

So had Gil's backpack.

Four

Gil didn't hesitate. Everything he owned in the world was in that backpack. Not only his spare clothes and toothbrush, but his penknife and his wallet with nineteen dollars and fifty cents inside, and a photo of his parents at Niagara Falls, and the yellow pebble, of course. With the hole through the middle.

He scrambled out of the SUV and crawled behind a large rubbish bin, his breath ragged. Whoever had stolen his backpack must surely be close by, but it was too dark to see anything.

An owl hooted so suddenly it made him jump. He peered around the side of the bin. The driver of the SUV was still visible in the headlights, although the dog seemed to have disappeared.

'Where did you go?' she asked, her voice sad. 'I wouldn't have hurt you...' She placed the rest of the sandwich on the ground and waited for a hopeful second or two. Then she turned away, defeated.

I've got ten seconds, Gil thought frantically. Ten seconds to get back into the SUV before it drove off. Yet he couldn't bear leaving his backpack behind.

As he hesitated, he heard the door of the SUV slam shut. He'd missed his chance. The driver was already accelerating away. Gil considered running after her, although he knew it was useless. She would never see him.

He was stranded.

It was very quiet, so quiet he could hear the creak and rustle of things shifting behind the black wall of trees. High in the sky, the moon shone with a fitful light, battling fast-moving clouds. He had no way of telling where he was, and not the slightest idea of what to do next.

Gil's eyes prickled, yet he was far too frightened to cry. He stood for a long moment; his arms wrapped tightly around his body. Then, not knowing what else to do, he began to walk towards the rest-stop exit.

It was late. The traffic had dwindled to a trickle. Whole minutes passed before the next pair of headlights broke the distant dark. But there was enough light from the moon for Gil to make out the motorway, in both directions. The lanes were joined, although he could see that they divided a little further along, curving around a large, central area. Gil guessed it was one of those green spaces often found in the middle of motorways.

The owl hooted again, more distantly this time. There was something odd about the sound. As if it wasn't really an owl, but more like…

Before he had time to finish the thought, two figures emerged from the shadows twenty metres away. He recognised the first immediately. It was the dog. There was no mistaking that long, sharp snout. The second figure was slight with an oddly humped back. A kid, perhaps, although he couldn't tell if it was a boy or a girl. The pair paused on the side of the road, then raced across the lanes, making for the green space in the middle. Just then, the moon broke through the clouds and Gil saw the two of them clearly.

The kid with the dog was a boy, with dark hair sticking up in spikes, and it wasn't a hump that he had. It was Gil's backpack.

'Hey!' Gil yelled. The headlights of an approaching car lit the darkness, and he crouched low, waiting for it to pass, then got to his feet and began to run as fast as he could towards where the two figures had disappeared. He reached the spot where they had crossed the motorway and stopped, half-terrified to set foot on the forbidden tarmac.

It was empty. There was nothing to fear. He dashed across, feet thudding, his nostrils full of the burned smell of the road. On the other side, the ground dipped without warning, and he tumbled headlong into deep grass. He staggered to his feet, gasping. Ahead of him rose a barrier of trees, thick with tangled bushes. Gil found an opening and plunged recklessly into the undergrowth.

Within a few steps he was in complete darkness. Even the sky had disappeared. He took a few, faltering paces, clutching blindly at branches, all sense of direction lost. Then his head slammed into the trunk of a tree and he fell.

Five

'He's dead,' a voice said.

'No, he isn't,' said a second voice, deeper than the first.

'Well, you'll have to kill him, then.'

'Why me?'

''Cos I said it first.'

Gil opened his eyes. He was lying face down, his cheek pressed against the ground, his forehead throbbing with pain. Close by, he could see the beam of a torch and two pairs of feet. The first in ragged trainers, the other – much larger – in leather shoes, battered and missing their laces. Neither of their owners wore socks.

'Only one way to decide,' the first voice said. There was the soft bump of fists, one-two-three.

'Rock!' both voices said together. Their fists bumped again.

'Scissors!'

'Stop doing that!' the first voice said.

'Doing what?'

'The same thing *I'm* doing!'

'Okay.'

Their fists bumped for a third time.

'Paper!' the voices said in unison.

A frustrated silence fell. 'I give up,' the first voice said at last. 'If we don't kill him, what *are* we going to do with him?'

Gil staggered to his feet. 'You took my backpack!'

The beam of the torch swung to his face, dazzling him. Gil shaded his eyes. It was the boy he'd been chasing; he was certain of it. The other figure was much taller, the height of a man.

'You took my backpack!' Gil repeated, although his throat was so dry, he could barely get the words out. Dizziness swept over him.

'I need something to drink,' he whispered, his legs buckling. 'I haven't had anything to drink for hours and hours…'

When Gil woke up next morning, everything had turned orange. The sight was so bizarre that, for a second or two, he couldn't move or even think. Then his mind cleared. He was in a tent.

Vaguely, Gil remembered stumbling over roots and fallen branches, following the bobbing torchlight through the trees, his head aching. At last, they'd stopped and he'd heard the sound of liquid pouring. A metal cup was pushed into his hand.

The water was warm and slightly musty, but Gil gulped it down as if he had never tasted water before, or known it existed up till then. After he'd drained two cups, he'd crawled into the tent – no more than a shape in the dark – and instantly fallen asleep.

He gazed at the light filtering through the orange nylon. Gil had never slept in a tent, and he immediately decided he liked it. It made him feel adventurous and cosy at the same time. *Perhaps a little too cosy*, he thought, struggling to sit up. The tent was so crammed with objects that there was barely room for him to move. There was a tyre, and a collection of battered hubcaps, but most of the items were pieces of luggage, including a shiny pink vanity case and a bag of golf clubs.

A bird gave a whistling call, and in the silence that followed, he heard the noise of traffic. Gil knew the road couldn't be far away, yet it sounded distant, almost unreal, like the muffled roar of a seashell held to his ear. With great difficulty, he squirmed to the front of the tent and peered cautiously through the flap.

There was another tent to his left – it was blue – and ahead of him a wide, grassy meadow, starry with wildflowers, their colours luminous in the dawn. Behind, a line of trees formed a screen so dense that nothing could be seen beyond it, apart from a few splinters of sunlight piercing the upper branches. In front of the tents was an area of flattened earth, and seated on a couple of upturned tin cans, were Gil's companions of the night before. At their feet was a camping stove; its tiny flame trying – with valiance but little result – to heat a pot of water.

The pair appeared much less alarming in the light of day. The smaller boy was extremely thin, almost puny, and the spikes in his hair – sticky with gel – were now squashed flat to the side of his head, where he'd been sleeping.

The other boy, who Gil had taken for a man, was certainly tall enough to be an adult. But there was something soft about his face, an almost babyish roundness, that made Gil suspect he was younger than he seemed. He sat awkwardly on his tin perch, all feet and knees, his broad shoulders hunched, as though ashamed of their own size.

Gil crawled through the tent flap and stood up.

'Where's my backpack?'

The smaller boy glanced at him and scowled, then jerked his head towards a couple of large barrels. Gil's backpack was wedged between them. He grabbed it and quickly searched the contents.

'Where's my penknife?'

'What penknife?'

'It was in my backpack!'

The smaller boy stared at Gil, his face blank.

'It's in his pocket,' the tall boy said without removing his gaze from the pot of slowly heating water.

'Eighteen blades and tools!' the smaller boy

exclaimed, reluctantly tossing the penknife to Gil. 'Who'd you steal it from?'

'I didn't steal it. I bought it.'

It wasn't often that Gil was given money, although he'd received a weekly allowance at a couple of his foster homes. It had taken him nearly a year to save up for the penknife, and he still wasn't sure why he'd wanted it so much. Perhaps because it gave him the feeling of being prepared. That no matter how upsetting the situation, or how worrying the problem, the penknife would have a tool that could fix it.

'Eighteen!' the boy repeated in a tone of undisguised envy.

'My favourite is the magnifying glass,' Gil admitted.

'Makes sense,' the boy said, nodding solemnly. 'Good for starting fires, a magnifying glass.'

Gil was about to tell him that starting fires wasn't something he did as a rule, but he decided against it.

'I know what you're thinking,' the boy said. 'You're wondering whether we're gonna let you stay, aren't you?'

'Stay where?' Gil asked.

'Where d'you think? Here, of course.'

Gil gazed at the tents and the meadow, and then to where the ground rose in a gentle slope towards an area dense with reeds. Beyond it, nothing but a green blur running uphill to distant trees. There was no sign of the road. The vegetation grew too thickly on every side. But Gil knew it was there, circling them like the sea, the sound of traffic as steady as waves against the shore.

'You mean, you *live* here?' Gil said. 'In the middle of the motorway?'

'No need be snotty about it,' the small boy said. 'You got any better place to live?'

Gil returned the penknife to his backpack, his head down.

'Didn't think so,' the boy said.

Six

The boys were called Riley and Grayson. Riley was eleven, and Grayson had just turned thirteen. They were brothers.

'Brothers?' Gil repeated.

'Don't start, I've heard it all before.' Riley's voice took on a mocking tone. *'Are you sure he's not your uncle? What happened, he ate all your food? Wow! I never knew Antman and the Hulk were related!'*

'I wasn't going to say anything like that,' Gil protested.

'Well, what, then?'

'I don't know,' Gil said, feeling ashamed.

'So, you said, "Brothers?" for no reason?'

'The water won't boil if you keep on arguing,' Grayson said, in his calm, deep voice.

Gil didn't understand how the two things could be related, although it was strange how the moment they stopped talking, bubbles began to cluster at the bottom of the pot.

'What are you making?' Gil asked.

'Coffee,' Grayson said. 'We're rationing the sugar and the powdered milk, so you'll have to drink it black.'

'That's how I always drink it,' Gil said, although he'd never tasted coffee in his life before. He'd always thought it was something that only adults drank, and he looked at Riley and Grayson with new respect.

'Where's Junk?' Riley said abruptly. 'Are there any beans left for him?'

'Half a can.' Grayson gestured towards a nearby tree. 'I wedged it in that branch, so he couldn't get at it.'

'Who's Junk?' Gil asked, although he'd already guessed. Either the dog had been watching them the entire time, or he was able to read their minds, for he was there as if by magic, almost vibrating with anticipation as he stared up at Riley.

'We found him on the side of the road,' Riley said. 'That's why he's called Junk. 'Cos someone threw him away.'

'They must have been crazy,' he added. 'I mean, just *look* at him!'

Gil *was* looking. In fact, he could hardly tear his eyes away. He hadn't realised, the night before, how ugly the dog was. It wasn't just his hairless tail, or his tiny, muddy eyes, or even his unpleasantly sharp, beak-like nose. It was the dreadful fact of his fur. The animal was yellow. Not golden-yellow, not the yellow of sand or butter, but a sickly, greenish shade, the colour of…

Pus, Gil thought.

'He's... different,' he said, glancing nervously at Riley.

'I know, right?' Riley smiled proudly. 'I figure he's one of those rare, fancy breeds. You know, that win medals and stuff at dog shows.'

'Yeah, must be,' Gil said, trying his best to sound as if he meant it. 'He's rare, all right...'

Riley fetched a hubcap and tipped in the leftover beans. It was a meagre breakfast, but the dog fell on it as if it were prime steak, devouring it in seconds. He licked the hubcap long after the last trace had gone, as though reliving a delicious memory.

'It's hard to imagine now,' Riley commented, 'but he looked really gross when we found him. All scabs, wasn't he, Gray?'

'Took ages to heal,' his brother agreed.

Gil looked from one to the other with rising disbelief.

'How long have you *been* here?' he said.

'Gray can tell you that,' Riley said. 'He keeps the calendar. It was his idea. Every morning, first thing, he cuts a mark in a stick. How long is it now, Gray?'

'Three weeks and two days,' Grayson said.

Seven

They had run away from home in a stolen car, Riley
told Gil as they drank their coffee. There were only two
tin mugs, but after rummaging for a few minutes in the
orange tent, Grayson emerged with a plastic McDonald's
cup, its logo faded to a shadow by the sun. As soon as
the coffee was poured, he disappeared for a second time,
returning moments later with a second hubcap filled
with fresh blueberries. He placed it on the ground by
the stove, and Riley produced a bag of battered-looking
crisps which he added to the berries, stirring the mixture
slowly and carefully, as if performing a ritual. Both boys
were silent as he did this, staring at their food in much
the way that Junk had stared at his beans, Gil realised.
With the same look of concentration in their eyes.

But he was staring too, his whole body hollowed
out by hunger.

Riley handed him the brimming hubcap. 'Four
berries and one chip,' he said. 'Then you pass it on.

That's the rule. It goes around until there's nothing left.' He narrowed his eyes. 'Got it?'

Gil nodded. The berries were large, with a dusty bloom on their dark blue skin, their flavour – sharpened by the tang of salty crisps – just the right mixture of sweet and tart. He filled his mouth and obediently passed the hubcap to Grayson.

Riley had stolen the car from the car park of a shopping mall and swapped the plates with the ones on his dad's Toyota, knowing that nobody would notice. The Toyota had been sitting in their backyard so long that weeds were growing out of the bonnet. After that, Riley – who Gil was starting to think must be some sort of criminal mastermind – had swiped his dad's credit card and withdrawn all the money in his account. It came to $980, and the boys had used it to buy camping equipment and as much food as they could fit into the stolen car. They had left the same day, before their dad got home from work. Grayson had done the driving.

'How'd you learn how to drive?'

'YouTube,' Grayson said.

'Everyone used to think Gray was stupid,' Riley said. 'Turns out they're the stupid ones.'

'But why did you do it?' Gil asked. 'Why'd you run away?'

Riley glanced at his brother without answering, and for a moment or two, the only sound was the shuffle of berries as the hubcap passed from hand to hand.

'I don't see why we have to tell you anything,' Riley said at last. 'We haven't even decided if you can stay or not.'

Gil thought of how he'd felt when the SUV had driven away, leaving him with nowhere to go and nobody to turn to. 'I want to stay,' he said, trying to keep the pleading out of his voice. 'I really, really want to.'

'We've already used up nearly half our food. That's why we're rationing stuff.'

'I don't eat much,' Gil said. 'I can survive on practically *nothing*.'

'What if you don't like it here and you leave? How do we know you won't rat on us?'

'I won't, I swear.'

'Easy to say. Doesn't mean anything unless you swear *on* something, does it, Gray?'

His brother paused, a handful of berries halfway to his mouth, his face blank as he thought. 'A Bible,' he said finally. 'You're meant to swear on a Bible.'

'That's right!' Riley's voice was mean with triumph. 'You got a Bible?'

Gil shook his head.

'What *have* you got, then?'

Gil reached into his backpack and brought out the photograph of his parents at Niagara Falls.

'What about this?' he asked, passing it to Riley.

'This your mum and dad?'

'Yeah,' Gil said softly.

Riley examined the photo silently, then gave Gil a long look.

'They're dead, aren't they?' he said.

'Yeah,' Gil said even more softly.

Riley nodded. 'What do you think?' he asked his brother. 'You think this is okay?'

'Yeah, it's okay,' Grayson said.

'You're lucky Gray's a nice person,' Riley told Gil, handing him back the photo. 'I guess you're in.'

'I'm in? But don't I have to swear?'

'Nah,' Riley said, suddenly not meeting his eye. 'We're good.'

There were three blueberries left. They each took one, and then Grayson wiped the empty hubcap with a handful of grass. Gil was surprised by how satisfied he felt after such a peculiar breakfast. He understood now, why Riley hadn't simply divided the food into three portions. It wasn't that taking it in turns to eat from the same dish made it last longer. Somehow, it also turned it into a proper meal, even though it was only a pile of berries and a few potato chips.

He looked with new curiosity at his companions, trying to figure them out. Riley talked a lot, and most of what he said sounded angry or mean. He acted like the leader. But it was strange how he seemed to do whatever Grayson wanted, even though his brother rarely spoke.

'Would you really have killed me?' Gil asked. 'Last night, when I was chasing you and hit my head?'

'You mean, if Gray hadn't cheated by reading my mind while we were playing Rock, Paper, Scissors, so we kept doing the same thing as each other?'

Gil nodded.

Riley gave him a hard stare. 'Definitely,' he said.

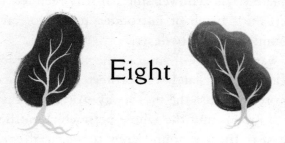

Eight

After breakfast, Gil was given a tour of his new home, yet neither Riley nor Grayson could tell him where it lay on a map. They weren't even sure what state they were in, let alone the name of this particular patch of ground. They simply called it 'the island', and it soon became clear to Gil how they had managed to live there for so long.

It was the perfect hideout.

Although ten thousand vehicles a day passed its shores, none ever stopped because stopping wasn't allowed on that stretch of motorway. The speed of the traffic and the treacherous curve of the road made it too dangerous. And it was even more unlikely that anyone might reach it on foot. Nobody walked along motorways for fun or crossed lanes of hurtling traffic on a whim. Occasionally, maintenance workers must come to tidy the edges and trim overhanging branches from the trees, but they had no reason to step any deeper inside.

The island had been created years and years ago when the motorway was first built. It had been almost completely ignored ever since. It had been left to run wild. Like a patch of untrodden jungle, or an oasis surrounded by empty desert.

It wasn't until Gil entered the screen of trees that he realised the island was protected from discovery by more than just the motorway. Although the trees (which ran around the whole perimeter) muffled the noise of traffic, the sound grew to a roar after only a few paces inside. Two steps further and Gil glimpsed the metal flash of passing cars. Another step and he could look right into the cars themselves, near enough to see the faces of the drivers and the trinkets dangling from their rear-view mirrors.

'Don't worry,' Riley said, as Gil shrank back in alarm. 'You can get way closer than that. They won't see you.'

'Why not?'

'Because they're not looking.'

Gil thought about all the times he'd been in Ms Lundy's car. Riley was right. Nobody looked at anything when they were on the motorway, except the road ahead. The exit ramps and verges and green areas passed in a blur, nothing more than places in-between, as interesting as the blank walls of a corridor. Cars travelled along motorways at all hours of the day and night, but they weren't really *there*.

They were merely on their way to somewhere else.

The island was in plain sight, impossible to miss. Yet it was invisible.

The tour took over an hour. They started in the boys' camp which was at the bottom of the island, where the ground was the flattest. It consisted of the two tents, a fire pit edged with stones, a washing line draped with a couple of T-shirts which had apparently been cleaned, although nobody would have guessed it by looking at them, Junk's 'kennel' – a wobbly-looking structure made from sticks, and two huge barrels filled with rainwater.

The water in the barrels was okay to drink, Riley told Gil. But the water in the pond further up the island needed to be boiled.

'You'd better not forget that,' Riley said, with a menacing look. 'Last thing we need is you getting sick.'

'What's the stuff in my tent?' Gil asked. 'All that luggage and the golf clubs. Did you bring that with you?'

Riley grinned. 'Not exactly.'

'Where did it come from, then?'

'You'll have to ask Junk that,' Riley said, his grin widening. 'He's not a pet, you know. He's a *working* dog.'

'You mean…?' Gil broke off as understanding dawned. He remembered the night before; the way the dog had kept his distance yet stayed close enough to entice the driver out of her SUV. And the way he'd moved, hobbling as though in terrible pain…

Gil glanced at Junk. The dog wasn't even limping now. Instead, he was busy digging a hole, his front legs sending clods of earth flying in every direction.

'You mean… it's just a trick?'

'Your face!' Riley cried, bursting into laughter.

'You stole that stuff in the tent from cars, didn't you? Like you tried to steal my backpack!'

Riley was laughing too much to reply. He cupped his hands to his mouth and hooted like an owl, then collapsed into hilarity again. Even Grayson was smiling. Gil thought of the traffic flowing around them, the ocean sound it made.

'You're like pirates.'

'Pirates!' Riley echoed in delight. '*Pirates*! That's exactly what we are. We ought to make a flag. Why didn't we think of that, Gray?'

'It's still stealing,' his brother said.

Riley turned down the corners of his mouth. 'Gray doesn't like it,' he told Gil. 'He says I can only take stuff from expensive-looking cars.'

'I agreed to that, of course,' he added hastily, not wanting to give the impression that he took orders from anyone. 'I mean, it makes sense. Only the expensive cars have anything *worth* stealing.'

'But why the golf clubs?'

'It's not like picking things out in a shop!' Riley snapped. 'It takes split-second timing.'

'So basically, you grab whatever you find.'

'Something like that,' Riley admitted. 'But I've got some good things. Boxes of groceries, a shovel, the sleeping bag in your tent, soap, shampoo…You'd be amazed what people leave lying around in the back of their cars.'

'How did you train Junk to limp?' Gil asked. 'You've only been here for three weeks.'

'He already knew how to do it,' Riley said, his voice filling with pride. 'Told you he's a champion.'

After Gil had seen everything there was to see in the camp, they headed across the meadow. The island was larger than most motorway green spaces. About the size of a couple of football fields, Gil guessed, although it looked even bigger because of all the trees and bushes, and because the slope of the ground hid the far end from view.

Wading through the meadow, still damp with dew, it was easy to forget they were in the middle of a busy motorway. The smell of the road – a mixture of petrol fumes and hot rubber – was much fainter than Gil expected. A host of other scents had taken its place. The herby smell of grass and growing wood, the perfume of flowers, the rich aroma of the earth itself. Even the sound of traffic had faded. Instead, a strange humming filled the air. Not the monotonous drone of machinery, but a living, pulsing sound, the voice of a multitude.

Insects, Gil thought. He'd never in his life been so aware of them. Barely a couple of metres from where he stood, a cluster of tiny white moths flickered above the grass. Bees bowed the head of every flower. Two butterflies – impossibly large and impossibly blue

– crossed and recrossed the meadow in a slow-winged dance. And these were just the creatures that Gil could see. The ground was alive with hidden movement, the leap of crickets, the creep of ants and the sturdy trundle of beetles great and small.

'How come there are so many bugs?' he asked.

'No pesticides,' Grayson said. 'Nobody cutting the grass and pulling up weeds.'

'It's not just bugs,' he added. 'There's snakes here too and birds I've never seen before. I saw a parrot yesterday, only it flew away. Must have been someone's pet.'

'If it comes back, I'll get it to sit on my shoulder,' Riley said, still thinking about pirates.

'Bats too,' Grayson continued. 'And tadpoles and frogs in the pond.'

Gil glanced at him. It was the most the older boy had said all morning. Grayson squared his shoulders as he spoke. He looked like a different person. Not huge and awkward and shambling, but tall and strong instead.

'It's like in that story,' Grayson said. 'Where the different animals get on a boat and get saved. This place is like that boat.'

'Noah's Ark?' Gil said.

'Noah's Ark?' Grayson repeated. 'Oh… I guess.' He stared at the ground, his shoulders returning to their usual dejected slump. 'I always thought it was Nowhere Sark,' he muttered. 'That's what it sounded like…'

'It *ought* to be "Nowhere" instead of stupid "Noah",' Riley burst out, rushing to his brother's defence. 'And "sark" is a word, right?'

'I don't think so,' Gil said.

'It's short for "sarcasm",' Riley insisted. 'As in "I don't need any more of your *sark*."'

'You made that up!' Gil said. 'What kind of a name is Nowhere Sark anyway?'

'How about Nowhere Island?' Grayson said, trying to avoid another argument. 'Why don't we call it that?'

'Genius!' Riley exclaimed.

Gazing at the secret life teeming around him, Gil had to agree.

As a name, Nowhere Island was perfect.

Nine

At the edge of the meadow, before the ground began to slope uphill, they came to the pond that Riley had mentioned. Although narrow and muddy, it was deep in the middle and surrounded by tall, thickly clustered reeds.

'I thought you said we couldn't drink from here,' Gil said, noticing a battered thermos flask wedged between two stones.

'It's for going to the bathroom.' Riley gestured further up the hill. 'There's a place there, in those bushes. Nice and private. We dug a hole. When you need to go, you fill the flask from the pond, and when you're finished, you use half the water to wash your butt.'

'With your hands?'

'No, Einstein, your feet,' Riley said. 'Of course, with your hands! It's way less messy than using leaves.'

'What do you use the rest of the water for?'

'How else are you going to get your hands clean?'

Riley rolled his eyes. 'After you're done, you take the flask back and leave it at the pond for the next person. Got it?'

Gil nodded.

'You'd better have. Forget to bring the flask back and you'll find yourself walking the plank.'

It was astonishing how many plants were growing on the island. Almost everywhere Gil looked, he saw something new. Ferns and brambles and nettles, dandelions and daisies, trees of all shape and size. Riley and Grayson showed him the blueberry bushes where his breakfast had come from, and a patch of wild strawberries. Grayson searched among the leaves until he found one, more brightly red than any strawberry Gil had ever seen before, and ten times sweeter.

There were also two apple trees, a peach tree, and a thorny clump that Grayson thought might be a blackberry bush. Who knew how their seeds had got there, whether blown by the wind, or tossed from a car. They had arrived on the island like everything else, simply by chance.

The boys showed Gil the lookout tree whose topmost branches gave a view of the rest stop further down the motorway. Grayson sat watch there when Riley and Junk went on their thieving expeditions. He had been up there last night, close enough to hear the thud when Gil hit his head.

'Sounded like it hurt,' he said.

Gil rubbed his forehead. There was still a lump, although the pain had mostly gone.

The stolen car was hidden not far away. The boys had pushed it deep into the bushes and covered it with branches.

'That's where we keep our food,' Riley said. 'I learned what we'd need from watching *Survivor*.'

The car was a dark green station wagon, neither new nor particularly old, the sort of vehicle that a family might own, Gil decided. Kids in the back seat, a dog in the far back and a bike or two strapped to the roof. Apart from a few dents and scratches it seemed none the worse for its adventure.

'What happened? You ran out of petrol?'

Grayson shook his head. 'I fell asleep.'

'It wasn't his fault,' Riley said. 'We'd been driving for hours, and it was really late at night, and he was only asleep for, like, three seconds.'

Luckily, the car had slowed to a crawl by the time it veered off the motorway. It rolled across the verge, scraped a tree and came to a stop in a patch of nettles. The boys had been too tired to try getting it back on the road that night. Instead, they'd pushed it further into the undergrowth and found a place to pitch their tent beyond the trees.

It had always been their plan to camp out in a remote spot. And they soon realised – as Gil had done – that the island was an ideal place. It wasn't just that it was hidden by trees and protected by the barrier of the motorway. The boys also knew it was possible because someone was already living there when they arrived.

It was a girl. Riley didn't know how old she was. Thirteen, perhaps.

'What happened to her?' Gil asked, astonished. 'Where did she go?'

'Nowhere,' Riley said. 'She's still here.'

'*Where?*'

Riley pointed to a thicket of trees beyond the meadow, a little to the left of the pond. 'She doesn't bother us, and we don't bother her,' he said. 'We call her Pez, but that's not her real name. Don't know her real name. Don't know anything about her at all.'

'How come? Didn't you ask?'

''Course we did. But she wouldn't answer. She wouldn't say anything, would she, Gray?'

'Not a single word,' his brother agreed.

Ten

At that moment, the girl they called Pez was squatting on her heels peering into a plastic tub full of crickets and looking a little like a cricket herself – all spindly arms and long, thin legs.

The boys had given her the name because there was a Pez dispenser with the head of Wonder Woman on the T-shirt that she wore as a dress, belted at the waist with an old leather strap. The T-shirt had once been bright, but it had long since faded to the colours of the earth, and the girl was almost invisible among the trees, her body as brown and gold as dappled sunlight.

She sat perfectly still, listening to the chirping song of the crickets, the tiny patter of their feet against the plastic tub. It was the third time she'd tried to collect the insects. On her first attempt, she'd covered the tub with a piece of fabric, tied around the rim with string, and on the second, she'd used slats from an old wooden crate. Both times the crickets had managed to creep away, their chirping dwindling steadily into silence.

Then, just the day before, she had found a pane of glass, a kilometre or two down the motorway. It was broken in half, but useable, and it made a fine lid for the tub. She had collected the crickets early that morning and not one had escaped. The girl counted them again with a feeling of satisfaction.

At the bottom of the tub, beneath an arrangement of twigs and leaves, there were two jar lids. One held water, the other was filled with soil for the crickets to lay their eggs. Crickets were a good source of protein, and the girl wanted them to breed. If they didn't, she would try something else, use different leaves, perhaps, or move the tub to a sunnier spot. Sooner or later, she would work it out.

The girl had a gift for working things out, although it was a gift she hadn't asked for and would have given back if she could, because it had brought her nothing but misery. It was why she was here, alone on an island in the middle of nowhere.

It was why her parents no longer loved her.

She fetched a rag and began furiously wiping the pane of glass, trying to rub the thought away.

The girl had never eaten crickets until she came to the island, but she had tasted plenty of other unusual things. She had been foraging for food and living off the land for most of her life. She knew how to trap animals and grow her own vegetables and which wild plants were safe to eat and which could be used for medicine.

It hadn't always been that way. She had lived in an enormous house when she was small. The girl could remember the huge carpets and the forest of chair legs in the dining room, and the watery shimmer of the swimming pool. Her parents had been rich then, so rich that they didn't need to work, and their lives were empty and without purpose.

Everything changed when the girl was four years old. They left the house and went to live on a farm with the Starborn. The farm was so old and so remote that not many people knew they were there, which is how the Starborn liked it. They didn't want any part of the outside world. They wanted to make their own rules, living for each other while they prepared themselves.

When the girl and her parents joined the group, there were about forty Starborn. Their leader was a woman called Juno Ray. She had lived a hundred lives and knew how to read the Maps of Heaven and she had an answer for everything. The Starborn loved Juno Ray and trusted her completely. It was terrible for the girl when she remembered that. It hurt her with a pain so deep and savage that her eyes would fill with tears, and she had to clutch herself to keep from sobbing. At these moments, the girl knew she had been right to run away.

She would never trust anyone ever again. She would live on her own for the rest of her life.

The girl finished cleaning the glass and stood up. The boys had passed by a little while ago, moving in their usual noisy fashion. The big one, feet thumping, the skinny one talking non-stop. She noticed a third boy had joined them, ordinary-looking, neither tall nor short.

The girl didn't think he would try to approach her. The others would tell him it was pointless. She remembered how they'd marched into her camp on their first day on the island. She was up in a tree long before they arrived, and she sat there, swinging her legs as the skinny boy shouted questions at her.

What's your name?

How old are you?

How long have you been here?

When she didn't answer, he repeated the questions, speaking slowly. After that, he'd resorted to mime; screwing up his face and pointing at this and that in a desperate effort to make himself understood.

She'd regarded him unblinkingly, waiting for him to give up. No matter how hard he tried she wouldn't talk to him or his brother – or to anyone else for that matter. Nobody could get to know her if she didn't speak, and nobody could become her friend. The day she left the Starborn, the girl had made a promise to herself.

She would never let anyone betray her again.

Eleven

As usual, Grayson had waited until dark to start the fire, when it was unlikely that any passing cars would see the smoke. As an extra precaution, he made sure the flames stayed low in the pit, well below the level of the ground. Just as at breakfast, the boys were silent as they prepared their evening meal, their eyes never leaving the pot that sat on a metal rack above the fire.

Supper was two packets of dried ramen noodles topped with an orange mush tasting vaguely of carrots.

'Is this baby food?' Gil asked, trying to work out the flavour.

'I didn't *know* I was stealing a nappy bag!' Riley burst out, in such an angry voice that Gil didn't dare to say that having had no lunch, he was happy to be eating anything. He simply nodded, and the hubcap passed from hand to hand until every scrap was gone.

'Here's the deal,' Riley announced, after the meal was over. 'We'll tell you why we ran away, and then you tell us why you did.'

'All right,' Gil said.

Riley's face took on a wooden look. 'Our dad hit us, okay. He didn't do it that often – maybe once a week – but then he started hitting us every day.'

'Why?'

Riley shrugged. 'I guess he got mad a lot.'

'What about your mum?'

'Gone,' Grayson said. And then, 'She was nice...'

A short silence fell.

'Your turn,' Riley said abruptly.

'But—'

'We told you, so now you tell us. That was the deal.'

Gil hesitated. 'I didn't really run away from home,' he said, stumbling over the words. 'It was more like I ran away from *no* home. Or maybe I just ran away from Ms Lundy, not because she was mean, it would've been easier if she was mean. It was because she was always so kind...'

'You're not making sense,' Riley told him. 'Start from the beginning.'

So, Gil did. At first the words came hesitantly, with many awkward pauses. But he soon lost himself in the telling of his story. He told about his life before his parents' accident. How few memories he had of that time, so that it felt like trying to rebuild a ruined palace with nothing but a few bricks and a handful of broken pottery. How he'd been placed in a foster home, not knowing it would be the first of many, and how even though the homes were different, they all made him feel the same way. Like a leftover. Like someone forever arriving at a party to which he hadn't been invited. Always on the outside, always hoping he'd be allowed to stay. Not knowing why he never was. Not knowing anything except what Ms Lundy would say as she drove him to yet another foster home.

I've got a good feeling about this, Gil. I'm sure it will be fine this time!

Riley and Grayson sat motionless, their eyes never leaving his face. Now Gil began to understand why they had been so quick to let him stay on the island, despite their diminishing store of food. After weeks with nobody except each other to talk to, they were eager for entertainment, however meagre.

When Gil began to describe how he'd escaped from Ms Lundy at the petrol station, Grayson's mouth fell open, and even Riley seemed impressed.

'You just got into a random car? *Badass!*'

'Don't stop!' he cried a moment later, as Gil came to the end of his story.

'There's nothing more to tell.'

'Tell us about something else, then.'

'Like what?'

'Anything,' Grayson said.

Gil thought for a while. 'I once saw a car – a Rolls Royce – going down the motorway at ninety miles per hour, with nobody inside.'

'Nobody?' echoed Grayson.

'It looked as though there was nobody, but then I saw the driver was an old woman. She was so tiny, she had to stretch her arms way up to reach the steering wheel. I doubt she could see more than three metres ahead.'

'Where was she going?' Riley demanded.

'She was running away from an old people's home.'

'How do you know? Are you making this up?'

'Stop interrupting,' Grayson said.

'The Rolls Royce was kind of tilted,' Gil continued. 'There was something heavy in the back seat. It was half a million dollars. The old lady was driving to Las Vegas as fast as she could to play the slot machines, so there'd be nothing left for her greedy family to inherit when she died. There was only one problem...'

Gil had always made up stories. But they had been to please himself. It had never occurred to him until now that they might please other people too. As he gazed at the expectant faces of the others, he felt a rush of sudden, mysterious hope.

Perhaps there was a place for him in the world, after all.

Twelve

After breakfast next morning, the three boys spent an hour sorting and organising the luggage in the orange tent to make more room for Gil. When that was done, Riley insisted it was time to teach him something that he called 'the drill'.

It was what to do if anyone came to the island and threatened to discover them. The warning call was a shrill whistle, followed by a dash to dismantle the camp. Gil was astonished by the speed and efficiency of the routine. In less than three minutes, the boys had kicked in the fire pit, removed the washing line, taken down the tents, and hidden their contents under a covering of branches. Even Junk had a role to play, vanishing into the undergrowth the instant he was given the command to hide.

After going through the routine several times, they managed – with Gil's help – to complete it in closer to two minutes than three, and they decided to take a break. Riley fetched half a bag of trail mix from the stores and proceeded to sort the ingredients into separate piles.

'I'll give you three raisins for an M&M,' he said, as soon as the piles had been equally distributed among them.

Grayson shook his head. 'Five.'

'Four.'

'Four and a peanut.'

Riley shook his head in mock disbelief. 'Four and *half* a peanut. That's my final offer.'

Gil's attention wandered. It was a warm day, the sky overcast, although there was a strange glitter to the clouds. A kind of prickling glare that made his head hurt, even when he looked away. He squinted. The glare had spread to the meadow. He could see every blade of grass, the petals on every flower…

'Hey,' Riley said, nudging him. 'I said, two peanuts for a cashew. Yes or no?'

'Okay,' Gil said, still staring at the meadow.

'You're meant to bargain. What's wrong with you? Cashews are worth at least five peanuts.'

'I guess I'm not hungry,' Gil muttered.

'What's wrong with you?' Riley repeated. 'You're not sick, are you?'

''Course I'm not,' Gil said, remembering Riley's dire warning about falling ill. 'I didn't drink any of the water in the pond…'

'Why are you shivering?' Grayson said, his face suddenly very close and very large.

'I don't know,' Gil said. 'I shiver sometimes. It's just something I do.'

He closed his eyes for a second, and when he opened them again, there was a halo over everything. From the largest tree to the tiniest leaf, every pebble, every tuft, even the butterflies flickering above the grass, were outlined in burning colour. Even more extraordinary than this, all the outlines were moving, vibrating together, as if to the beat of single heart. And Gil suddenly saw that there was no difference between tree and rock, no border separating land from sky. Everything was connected and everything was singing the same vast, wordless song.

'Can you hear it?' he said. 'Can you hear it?'

'Hear what?' Riley said from a long way away.

'The whole world's *alive*,' Gil whispered.

Gil lay for the rest of the day, and all the following night, in a narrow corridor between asleep and awake. The walls of the corridor were orange, close enough to touch, but his hands had grown to ten times their usual size, and he didn't have the strength to lift them.

Grayson put a wet cloth on his forehead, and Gil's mind cleared briefly.

'I didn't drink the pond water. I promise I didn't.'

'Doesn't matter,' Grayson said, so kindly that tears rose in Gil's eyes. 'Don't worry.' Grayson rubbed his arms and hands with the wet cloth until they went back to their normal size.

'My pebble,' Gil said. 'With the hole…'

'In your backpack?'

Shadows passed over the walls of the tent, each different. One had the head of a lion, another scuttled sideways like a crab. Gil held the pebble tight against his chest.

'What are we going to do?' someone said in a whisper outside the tent.

'What if he…?'

Grayson crouched over Gil with a drink. It had a dark, bitter taste, and he tried to push it away, but Grayson wouldn't let him until it was finished. He slept and woke and slept again, and when he woke for the second time, his fever had broken. It was morning. He lay quietly, basking in the simple joy of feeling well again, listening to the hum of insects and the murmur of voices beyond.

Grayson and Riley were sitting in their usual spot, a pot of water on the stove between them. Junk lay at their feet, his greyish tongue lolling out. The boys' faces lit up when Gil emerged from his tent, and Junk stirred and thumped his hairless tail.

'So, you decided to get up,' Riley said, trying – without success – to hide his relief. 'About time!'

'How do you feel?' Grayson asked.

'Great,' Gil said, moving on wobbly legs to sit beside them.

'You were *sick*,' Riley told him with relish. 'I thought you were a goner for sure. Gray kept giving you water and putting cloths on your head and stuff, but I told him not to bother. I said there wasn't any point, didn't I, Gray?'

Grayson opened a packet and tipped the contents into a tin mug. He added boiling water and stirred the mixture until it grew thick.

'Oatmeal,' he said, handing it to Gil, together with a plastic spoon. 'It's the last packet.'

'Maple syrup flavour,' Riley added, his eyes fixed longingly on the mug.

'It's good,' Gil said, taking a mouthful and then a second, larger one. '*Really* good…'

He broke off, the spoon halfway to his mouth. Junk was suddenly in front of him, his beady eyes following Gil's every move.

'He's using mind control on you,' Riley said. 'Junk's good at that. He's trying to make you eat so fast that you'll be sick.'

'Why?'

''Cos then he'll get to eat your throw-up.'

Gil swallowed nervously. 'I like your scarf,' he told Riley, to change the subject. The scarf was bright green silk. Riley was wearing it wrapped around his head and tied with a knot at the back.

'It's not a scarf. It's a *bandana*. I found it in one of the bags I stole. And here's something else I found.' He opened his hand and showed Gil a gold, hooped earring.

'Hardcore pirate, amiright? I can't wear it, though, because Gray won't pierce my ear for me. He says it'll get infected.'

'I said it *might*.'

'Not if we heat the safety pin!'

There were four or five spoonfuls of oatmeal left. Gil hesitated, struggling with himself. Then he gave the mug to Junk to lick clean. Riley was still arguing with Grayson about ear piercing.

'If you won't do it, Gil will. Right, Gil?'

'I don't know how…'

'You're too chicken!'

'I guess I am,' Gil said. 'Also, Grayson's right. It's not safe.'

'Now you're ganging up on me.' Riley looked from one face to the other. 'Fine!' he shouted. 'See if I care!'

He leaped to his feet and stomped away through the grass, Junk following faithfully at his heels.

'Did he really tell you not to bother looking after me when I was sick?' Gil asked Grayson. He tried to make his voice sound light, although Riley's comment had hurt him. He didn't know why Riley was so unkind. It was true that he could be friendly from time to time – after Gil had made the comment about pirates, for example – but his friendliness never lasted. Before long he was back to his old, sarcastic self. 'I guess he doesn't like me that much,' he said.

Grayson picked up a stick and began whittling it, peeling the bark carefully with his knife.

'It's not that,' he told Gil. 'It's that Riley *has* to be bad.'

'Why?'

Grayson whittled for a moment; his head bent. 'Because of our dad,' he said finally. 'Riley decided no matter how bad our dad was, he was going to be worse. If he was always the worst person around, nobody could ever get to him.'

Grayson began to carve a delicate line around the top of the stick. His hands were as large as the rest of him, his fingernails bitten to the quick and the surrounding skin ragged where he had worried it with his teeth. But he handled his knife with astonishing skill.

'Promise you won't say I told you,' he said, 'but Riley was so worried about you being sick that he was talking about stopping a car to get help for you.'

'That would have meant he'd be caught... sent back home, maybe.'

Grayson nodded.

'So why did he act like you were the only one who cared about me getting better?'

'Because that's what he wants you – wants everyone – to think. That he only does the right thing because I say so, d'you see? Means he always gets to stay the worst person...' Grayson paused; the knife frozen in his hand; his whole body paralysed with the effort of finding the right words.

'I'm good so he doesn't have to be,' he said at last, returning to his whittling with an air of relief. 'That's what it is.'

'Well, I'm glad I got better,' Gil said. 'Before you had to stop a car, I mean.'

'It was Pez got you better. Last night. She doesn't wear shoes, you know. She walks so quiet you don't hear her coming. I look up and she's standing there at the edge of the camp with a cup in her hand. Minute I take it, she's gone.'

'I *remember* you giving me something weird to drink…'

'We thought it was worth a try. If it didn't work we could always—'

He was interrupted by a sudden cry, half-whoop, half-scream. Riley was tearing through the meadow towards them, hand clapped to the side of his head.

'I did it myself!' he yelled, his voice bubbling with panicky triumph. 'I did it! I took the pin, *and I stuck it all the way through!*'

Thirteen

Pez was worried about the bird. He wasn't doing what birds were meant to do, even huge ones with bald, orangey-grey heads.

He had appeared weeks ago, a vast shape huddled at the base of a tree. He must have slipped from his perch and now, exhausted by hunger and pain, he barely moved when she approached. Pez had no idea where he had come from, although she guessed it was somewhere with a lot of mountains. It was certainly not from where she used to live. The Starborn's farm was in a part of the country where the land was completely flat for hundreds of miles in all directions. They'd chosen it because when they looked up at the night sky, there was nothing – not even a tree – to come between them and the stars. It made them feel as if they were standing on the very edge of the world and, with a single step, might cross to heaven.

Pez could see that one of the bird's legs was broken.

Perhaps in a collision with a power line, she thought. She'd set the leg as best she could, her hands trembling at the bird's size, the sharpness of his hooked beak, designed for tearing flesh. But he never stirred, allowing her to mend his leg and even smooth the dishevelled feathers at his neck with a look of patience in his rust-coloured eyes.

He was the politest of creatures, she decided. As though he knew he cut an alarming, shambling figure and wanted to make up for it. The first time she brought him roadkill – a flattened squirrel, freshly dead – he'd waited until dark before eating, as though to spare her the sight of his savage table manners. Not a day went by where he didn't spend at least an hour or two vigilantly grooming his feathers to remove any trace of dust and food.

Pez wished she had more information about the bird. Did he live on his own, she wondered, or was he part of a flock? What kind of egg had he hatched from? How much distance could he travel in a single day?

She had always loved facts and figures. There had been a sparse collection of children's books on the Starborn's farm, and she had enjoyed them all when she was younger. But her favourites had been the non-fiction titles. There were three of them. *Incredible Insects*, *The Solar System* and *How Weather Works*. Pez knew them almost by heart.

'You want the insect book *again*?' her dad would say as he tucked her into bed. 'You've heard it a hundred times.'

'Read the stuff about tarantulas,' Pez said. 'It's on page twenty-two, remember?'

Her dad gave a sigh. 'Tarantulas it is, then…'

The bird's broken leg had healed a while ago, and when he spread his wings – their underside as wide and as white as a range of snow-capped peaks – Pez could see there was nothing stopping him from flight. Yet he stayed. Lumbering to and fro on foot, never venturing beyond the shelter of her camp.

That morning, he'd spent even longer than usual grooming himself, washing and preening with unflagging zeal. Now he sat beside her, apparently exhausted, his blotchy head – naked as a turkey's – tucked beneath his wing. Pez leaned towards him, resting her own head against his soft, black bulk.

He needs to go back to where he came from, she thought. *He needs to fly home.*

She heard a sound and was on her feet in the blink of an eye. Someone was coming. Pez hesitated, then made her silent way to the edge of the trees that surrounded her camp. It was the boy. The new one.

'Hello?' he called, his voice uncertain.

'Hello? Hel—' He broke off, catching sight of her. 'I came to say th-thank you,' he stammered. 'For helping me get better.'

Pez stared at him, her face stony, willing him to go away.

'I brought you a present.' He placed something on the ground and hastily stepped back.

Pez knew she ought to ignore him, but curiosity got the better of her. Without taking her eyes off the boy, she went and picked up the object, feeling the weight of it in her hand.

'It's a bottle in the shape of the Eiffel Tower,' the boy told her. 'Ms Lundy – my social worker – went to France on holiday, and she gave it to me when she got back. She said she wanted to get me something better, only there wasn't much to choose from at the airport.'

Pez risked a quick look at the bottle.

'It used to have bubble bath in it,' the boy said, sounding apologetic.

Pez put the bottle down and turned away, not looking back until she was safely in the shadow of the trees. He was still standing there. As if he didn't know what to do next.

'I was hoping I could come to see your camp,' he said, although his voice was more resigned than hopeful.

Pez was about to shake her head, but something stopped her. Perhaps it was the way his face had fallen when she'd put the bottle down. She stared at him for a second or two, then shrugged and turned her back again, pretending not to notice when he followed.

I won't talk to him, she thought. *It's okay if I don't talk.*

She reached the clearing where she'd made her camp and began tidying up the fire pit, brushing ash and rearranging stones without glancing once in the boy's direction. But she could sense him taking everything in. The tub of crickets, the interwoven branches of her tepee, the climbing rope hanging from the hollow tree, and beyond the tree, the tidy plot – green with new leaf – where she had planted vegetables in careful rows.

'Wow,' the boy said. 'Wow.'

At the sound of his voice, the bird woke with a start, raising his head from his wing so rapidly that the ruff of feathers around his neck quivered.

'What's *that*?' the boy cried. 'Is that a… *condor*?'

The bird shifted from foot to foot with an air of embarrassment. Then he ducked his head and shuffled heavily away, making for the grass-lined dip where he liked to roost.

'How did a condor get here?' the boy said. 'Where did it come from? Why doesn't it—' He broke off. 'I forgot, you don't…'

'Maybe you don't speak English,' he said. *'Hablas Espanol? Aprendi Espanol de mis padres…'*

Pez carried on tidying the fire pit, watching him from the corner of her eye. He picked up a stick and began scratching letters in a patch of bare earth.

Can u read and write?

Pez struggled with herself, but she couldn't resist the temptation.

No, she scratched.

At once she regretted it. The boy laughed. It wasn't a snigger or a chuckle, but a real, out-loud laugh that lit up his whole face.

'I'm Gil,' he said, still smiling.

Pez glared at him; her teeth clenched.

'What's the matter?' he said, his smile fading.

Pez's teeth were clamped so tight that her jaw ached. She kept glaring.

'I… guess I'd better be going.' The boy waited in uncertain silence for a moment. 'Well, bye, then,' he said with an awkward wave of his hand.

She watched him walk through the trees and disappear into the sunlight. It wasn't until he had completely vanished that she picked up the bottle he'd left for her.

Pez ran her fingers gently over the ridged glass. She unscrewed the top and brought the bottle to her nose. It smelled of soap, a memory of sweetness, faint and far away. She replaced the top and went to check on the crickets, although it was a while before she could bring her mind to focus on the contents of the tub.

She saw now that it had been a mistake to help the boy get better, even though she hadn't done anything particularly difficult. The remedy – a mixture of bog myrtle and crushed cornflowers – had been easy to prepare. But an even bigger mistake had been letting him visit her camp. It wasn't that she'd made him laugh – although that was bad enough.

It was the fact that a part of her – a small, foolishly hopeful part that even the Starborn hadn't managed to destroy – wanted to make him laugh again.

Fourteen

Not long after she'd stopped speaking, Pez had discovered something surprising. Her hearing had become ten times sharper, and her ears could pick up even the slightest of sounds. The march of ants and the settling of leaves, and all the different ways the rain fell. Before, she'd only been able to hear the words that people said. Now she could hear all the words they didn't say too.

That was how she knew what the boy called Gil wanted more than anything else in the world, even though all he'd talked about was her camp, and the bird, and the bottle in the shape of the Eiffel Tower.

What he wanted more than anything was to belong. To someone or to something.

Pez understood that. Her parents had been the same way. They'd never felt they truly belonged to anything until they joined the Starborn. That was what they had always told her.

The Starborn were not like other people. They were the great-great-great-great grandchildren of beings who had fallen from the stars. And one day they would return to where they came from. Nobody knew when that day would come, not even Juno Ray. But she told them it would be soon. In the meantime, they had to make themselves ready. They had to free themselves from everything to do with the world. Telephones and computers and art and whatever was happening in the news. The more they enjoyed something, Juno Ray said, the more important it was to give it up. Like listening to music, or owning pets, or growing flowers instead of useful things like vegetables.

Pez loved her parents, and she loved Juno Ray, so she did as she was told. Deep down, though, she felt worried and confused because she knew she didn't want to be free of the world. She liked it too much. She liked that the world had rules. Carrots grew from carrot seeds, chickens came out of eggs and weather could be predicted from the size and shape of clouds. The world made Pez feel that there was a reason for everything, and if she didn't know what it was, she could find out.

Once, when she was about six years old, she had rescued three tadpoles stranded in a puddle. She placed them in a jam jar and watched them transform, day by day, into tiny frogs. Their legs sprouted and their tails grew smaller and smaller until they vanished. Then one morning, Pez saw that they had changed colour overnight, from muddy brown to a shade of green so bright it was almost neon.

'Why did they turn that colour?' she asked her parents.

'I guess that's what frogs do,' her mum said.

'But why *that* colour? Why?'

Her dad shrugged. 'It's just the way it is…'

Pez wanted to find a home for the baby frogs, so she carried the jam jar to a pond that lay close to the farm. When she got there, she stopped in surprise. The water in the pond was normally clear. But spring had arrived, and the surface was completely covered with floating duckweed. Pez felt something widen in her mind, as if a door she hadn't even known was there had suddenly opened.

The duckweed was the exact same shade of green as her frogs.

That was why they'd turned that colour, she thought. To blend in and keep safe from creatures who wanted to eat them. Her dad hadn't been right when he'd said, 'It's just the way it is.'

For the first time in her life, it occurred to Pez that her parents didn't know everything.

After Gil had gone, Pez spent the rest of the afternoon weeding her vegetable plot and removing insects from the tender leaves. Now that the plants were well established, she no longer needed to water them every day. She had worked out that the earth was kept moist by rainwater seeping downhill, gathering in the places where the ground grew flat.

The potatoes were getting big. Pez dug with her hands and uncovered two particularly fat ones. She lit the fire and boiled them with a sprig of mint and a wild onion, and ate them with her fingers, straight from the pan. The potatoes tasted of earth, the way that freshly picked strawberries taste of sunlight, and fish taste of the wide blue sea. Pez lingered over the last few mouthfuls, relishing each morsel. Then she wiped the pan and stored it neatly in the hollow tree.

It was nearly dark. She sat with her hands clasped around her ankles and her chin on her knees, listening to the murmur of the insects and the night settling on the branches of the trees. A light breeze brought the smell of wood smoke. The boys had built their evening fire. Pez tilted her head and caught the crackle of kindling and the distant sound of voices.

She rose to her feet and crept through the trees, into the meadow, avoiding the path where the boys had flattened the grass on their way to and from the pond. When she had crawled as close as she dared, she dropped to her stomach and lay still, listening.

Fifteen

Grayson had washed his brother's ear first with hot water, and then with whisky – the dregs of a bottle tossed from a car – to sterilise the wound. Now Riley sat by the fire, his gold hoop gleaming in the flickering light, his face filled with the quiet pride of one who has glimpsed the jaws of death and lived to tell the tale.

Since Gil was sharing their food, Grayson had decided they needed to ration it even more carefully. Supper had been a meagre affair; a pan of rice mixed with precisely six dollops of ketchup – Riley had counted them out loud.

'I'd give anything for a burger,' Grayson said, running his finger around the bottom of the pan in case he had missed a grain of rice. 'A burger with cheese.'

'With extra cheese,' Riley said.

'And bacon.'

'With extra cheese *and* extra bacon.'

Food was always a popular topic of conversation

among the boys, particularly that evening after Gil had told them about Pez's vegetable plot.

'I forgot to tell you, she eats crickets,' Gil said, remembering the plastic tub. 'At least I think she does. I don't know why she'd keep them otherwise. Maybe we could do that too…'

'I *guess* we could,' Grayson said, after a moment of silence. 'But… not alive?'

'No,' Gil said hastily. 'No, 'course not, we'd cook them first.'

'Probably don't taste that bad,' Grayson said, swallowing. 'Maybe sort of… *crunchy*?'

'Can we talk about something else?' Riley cried.

'Like what?'

'Like your pebble,' Grayson said, looking at Gil. 'With the hole through it.'

Gil said, 'It's just a pebble.'

'If it's just a pebble, why'd you ask for it when you were sick?' Riley demanded. 'We couldn't get it out of your hands, could we, Gray?'

'I found it on a beach,' Gil said. 'A couple of years ago… you'll think it's stupid.'

'Yeah, probably,' Riley said. 'It's better than talking about eating crickets, though.'

Gil stared into the fire without saying anything.

'Tell us,' Riley ordered. '*Start!*'

'Okay,' Gil said. '*Okay*. I found it on a beach. It was at one of my foster homes. I was there for three months; I knew it was only going to be temporary. Ms Lundy told me that. The lady fostering me was called Helen.

She said she was a photographer, but I don't think she made much money because her house was kind of shabby. When it rained, she had to use a bucket to catch the drips from the leaky roof. It was great though because she lived right next to the ocean. I could see the beach from my bedroom window. Not many people came to the beach, it was really wide, and you had to walk for ages to get to the sea. But I liked it, and I liked Helen too. I liked her the best of all my foster parents.'

'What was so great about *her*?' Riley asked. 'She sounds kind of depressing to me.'

'Stop interrupting,' Grayson said.

Gil liked Helen because she neither ignored nor made a fuss of him. And, because when she asked him questions, it wasn't to be polite, or to test him, or to make him say what she wanted to hear. It was because she was truly interested in what he might tell her. Most of all, he liked Helen because she looked at everything, and when he was with her, he looked at everything too.

Each day at low tide, she would walk along the beach, near the edge of the water, where the sand was flat and wet and gleamed so bright you had to shade your eyes. She walked towards the distant cliffs until she was out of sight then she came all the way back again. The third day after he arrived, as she was about to set off, she saw Gil sitting on the front steps, picking at a splinter in the warped wood.

'Want to come beachcombing with me?'

'Beachcombing' turned out to be searching for things that the tide had left behind.

'What sort of things?' Gil asked.

'Anything interesting,' Helen said, bending to pick up a piece of twisty driftwood. 'There are often unusual shells on this beach and sometimes lovely glass buoys from old fishing nets. Once I found a wooden doll that was worn so smooth, it must've been floating in the ocean for a hundred years.'

Helen didn't just look for treasures on the beach, she looked at other things too, pointing them out to Gil as they went along. A pattern in the waves, a rock shaped like a bear, the way the sandpipers ran on spindly legs, chasing the retreating surf until it turned and chased them back again.

Walking on the beach with Helen made the world seem rich. As though all it needed was to be noticed.

'What's this got to do with your pebble?' Riley complained, shifting impatiently.

'I'm getting there.'

Pebbles with holes through them were called 'hagstones', Helen told Gil. She had never found any on this beach, although she was always looking because they were said to be lucky.

'Lucky in what way?' Gil asked.

'People used to think they protected you from harm, and that if you looked through one you might see Fairyland.'

'There's no such place.'

'Maybe not,' Helen said, smiling at him. 'Maybe they just meant you'd see a different world. A better one, perhaps.'

Gil knew it probably wasn't true. It was superstition. But after that conversation, he looked for a hagstone each time he walked along the beach. It wasn't until the last morning of his stay that he finally found one, although it was more like it found him. He glanced down and there it was, lying by his feet, in a spot he was sure had been empty the second before. He picked it up and ran to give it to Helen.

'I can't take it,' she said. 'It belongs to you. Besides, it's only lucky for the person who found it.'

Gil raised the hagstone to his eye. Looking through made everything seem nearer. And at the same time, it made everything seem further away.

'What can you see?' Helen asked.

Gil hesitated, not wanting to disappoint her. 'I don't see anything different, or better,' he admitted at last. 'It's the same old world.'

Helen smiled again, although her eyes were sad. 'Maybe you'll have to keep looking,' she said.

There was a silence after Gil finished speaking. Then Riley made a face.

'You were right, that *is* kind of stupid. It's not even a good story, is it, Gray?'

'Not really,' Grayson said.

'Nothing actually happened,' Riley persisted. 'Things have to happen in stories, don't they?'

'Think they're meant to,' Grayson agreed.

Another silence fell.

'Can I have a look at it?' Grayson asked. Gil dug for the pebble in the pocket of his jeans and placed it in Grayson's huge palm. He raised it solemnly to his eye and gazed through it for a while at the stars, before passing it to Riley.

Riley looked through the pebble at Junk, lying by the fire, his paws twitching as he dreamed. Then he looked into the fire itself, frowning in concentration. It was growing late. The sound of traffic had hushed, and all that could be heard was the hum of the earth and the dry whisper of the reeds around the pond.

'Stupid,' Riley muttered. '*Stupid…*'

Sixteen

It rained during the night, a steady pattering against the walls of the tent, too soft to disturb Gil's sleep. He only woke when it stopped, a little before dawn. He pulled on his trainers and crept outside. The sky was pale grey, as pearly as the inside of a shell, and raindrops hung suspended from the tips of the grasses.

Gil went to the water barrels, moving quietly so as not to wake the others. It was that time of day when the world feels mysteriously private, belonging only to those who are awake, and Gil wanted to keep it to himself for a while longer.

The barrels were full to the brim. Gil cupped his hand and drank, the water still cool from the night. He looked up.

A fox was standing four metres away, sniffing the ground near the remains of the fire. Gil knew it was a fox. It had the same slender, high-stepping legs, the same rust-coloured coat and brushy tail. Yet it was too small to be a fox. It was no bigger than a cat.

Gil stared at the creature, his hand transfixed mid-air. Perhaps it was some kind of stoat, or an odd-looking squirrel...

The fox must have sensed it was being watched, for it suddenly glanced in his direction, and to his astonishment Gil saw that its eyes were as blue as the summer sky. He caught his breath and then, between one heartbeat and the next, the fox was gone.

Gil didn't know why Riley had said he could join him on the thieving expedition that night. He didn't want to ask in case the other boy changed his mind. For the same reason, he didn't dare refuse when Riley tossed him the jar of hair gel after carefully teasing his own hair into spikes.

'I'm the leader on this mission,' Riley told him for the tenth time. 'You're not going to do *anything* unless I tell you.'

'I won't,' Gil said, mashing the gel against his scalp. 'I promise.'

'You look ridiculous,' Riley said. 'You look like you have horns.'

Gil tugged at his hair, trying to shape it.

'Now you look like a unicorn!'

Riley picked up a stick and began drawing lines in the damp earth. 'Okay, let's go through it one more time. Here's the island, and here's where we cross the road, just before the lanes join, do you see? And *here* –' Riley pointed the stick – 'is the rest stop, but we don't wait there. We wait further down the motorway so the cars will have plenty of time to see Junk and turn into the rest stop after him…'

'What if Junk gets caught?'

'Impossible,' Riley scoffed.

'Or you get caught.'

'Even more impossible.'

Grayson paused in his whittling. 'I'll be up in the tree, remember? I'll be watching the whole time.'

'We leave at two on the dot,' Riley told Gil. 'If you're late I'll go without you.'

It was a long wait. Gil's head itched terribly from the gel. He lay in his tent feeling more and more apprehensive as the minutes passed. By two a.m. he was so jumpy with nerves that he wanted to throw up. He crawled out of the tent and started with shock. Riley was right in front of him, grinning dementedly, his face thickly covered with mud.

'Camouflage.' Riley handed him a wet lump. 'Slap it on and don't forget your neck.'

Gil wondered if he was being pranked. But Riley was all business, a bag slung across his chest and Junk panting at his heels. Even before Gil had finished plastering his face with the mud, Riley was already making his way through the trees.

It was a windless night, the air thick and muggy, the motorway empty apart from a few late travelling cars.

Riley and Junk trotted swiftly across the tarmac and Gil hurried after, his feet thudding almost as loudly as his heart.

'It's like being followed by an elephant,' Riley hissed. 'Stop scratching your head. Pull yourself together.'

They followed the motorway in single file, keeping close to the trees, heading for the exit to the rest stop. Each time a car passed, they crouched automatically, Junk sinking to his belly without needing to be told. *Perhaps he really is a champion dog*, Gil thought, hard though that was to believe.

They turned into the rest stop and Riley switched on the torch strapped to his head.

'First thing I always do is check the rubbish,' he said, hurrying to the bin.

'I know what you're thinking,' he added.

'I'm not thinking anything,' Gil protested. 'I wasn't even *looking* at you.'

'Plenty of good things in rubbish bins,' Riley said, rummaging through the bags and empty tins.

'Almost half a burger!' he cried, tossing it to Junk. 'And another – only a couple of bites taken out!' Riley tucked it into his bag. 'That's for later, Junk.'

'A packet of salt, three packets of ketchup,' he continued, still searching. 'Car air freshener... might come in useful... old flip-flop... Who throws away a single flip-flop?'

'I dunno,' Gil said. 'Someone with only one foot?'

'Funny.' Riley reached deep into the bin and retrieved a plastic bag.

'Bingo!'

Whoever had filled the bag with snacks for their journey must have lost their appetite along the way. Riley pulled out three sticks of pepperoni and five of string cheese – all unopened – as well as a large bag of Doritos, three quarters full.

'Now that's what I call a good start to the night,' he said.

He switched off his torch and they kept walking, through the rest stop and out on to the motorway again. After a few metres, Riley stopped.

'This'll do.'

It was so dark that Gil could barely make out the edge of the road. He glanced back the way they had come. 'Can Grayson really see this far? Even up in the tree?'

''Course not.'

'Then why —'

'Get down,' Riley interrupted. 'Car coming.'

Gil saw headlights grow large above the trees, then the car turned a bend and was speeding towards them. Riley, flat on his stomach, cupped his hands to his mouth.

'Limp, Junk, *limp*!'

He had timed it perfectly. As the car came abreast, Junk was already nearly halfway back to the rest stop. Gil saw him in the headlights for a second, staggering pathetically along. Then the car swept by and left him in darkness.

'That was cold,' Riley said in disgust. 'They didn't

even slow down.' He hooted and Junk came bounding back. Riley hugged him tightly and gave him a Dorito.

'He'll do anything for food,' he said.

A truck thundered by. Riley shook his head.

'If Grayson can't see us, why does he go up the tree?' Gil asked as they waited.

Riley shrugged. 'I guess he's worried I'll get into trouble. Not that he'd be able to do anything even if I did. He's never been in a fight in his life, never even hit anyone. That's why we had to run away.'

'I thought it was because of your dad.'

Riley tugged angrily at a tuft of grass. 'Okay, I'll tell you. I said my dad hit us but that isn't true. He only hit Gray.'

'Why?'

'How should I know? Maybe because Gray never hit back. It made my dad mad. He kept on and on, trying to make him hit back. Gray wouldn't, but I knew he couldn't take it much longer. Sooner or later, he was going to thump my dad so hard he'd probably crack his skull.'

'So, you ran away before your dad got hurt?'

Riley clenched his fists. 'I didn't care if he got hurt! I just didn't want *Gray* to hurt him! Gray's the good one. Someone has to be the good one, can't you get that? I'm bad so *he* doesn't have to be!'

'That's weird,' Gil said, forgetting he'd promised not to repeat what Grayson had told him. 'He said almost the same thing about—'

'Car!' Riley interrupted. 'Nothing behind it. Get ready, Junk. I've got a good feeling!'

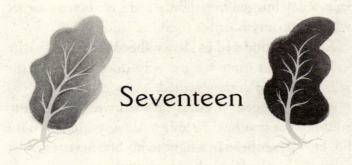

Seventeen

Gil crouched in the bushes at the edge of the rest stop. He couldn't see Riley, but he knew he was there, lurking behind the rubbish bin, waiting for a chance to strike.

The car – a jeep – had slowed the instant Junk appeared and had followed him into the rest stop. The driver was alone. He was a burly man, wearing a baseball cap several sizes too small, his hair sticking out over his ears. He squatted on his heels in the glare of the headlights, staring at Junk and making little clicking noises.

'Poor old fella, lost, are you?'

Gil felt bad. The man's voice was kind. He didn't deserve to be robbed. But Riley was already opening the back of the jeep. Ten seconds later he came scuttling back, lugging a large box by the handle. He waited for a moment to catch his breath, then gave Junk the signal to retreat.

'Hey,' the man cried. 'Where'd you go?' He walked

up and down, peering into the darkness, then took off his too-small cap and rubbed his head with an air of confusion.

The jeep disappeared and Gil joined Riley at the rubbish bin.

'It's a cooler,' Riley said, showing him the box. 'There was a bunch of fishing rods and this cooler.'

'Probably just bait.'

Riley switched on his torch and tugged the lid off the box.

'Steak!'

'What?'

'Steak!' Riley repeated, his voice rising to a squeal. 'Plus, corn, plus a watermelon... stuff for a whole barbeque. Bet you anything that guy's on his way to meet his fishing buddies. Imagine their faces when he turns up with nothing to eat!'

If Gil thought they would return to the island after stealing the cooler, he was wrong. The success seemed to have gone to Riley's head.

'I'm on a lucky streak,' he kept saying, as they resumed their waiting positions on the grass verge. 'I can feel it in my bones. Next car's gonna have a picnic hamper for sure.'

'It's the middle of the night,' Gil said, his head drooping with tiredness. 'Nobody goes on a picnic in the middle of the night.'

'That's why I've never found one. Until *now*.'

'Why'd you want a picnic hamper so bad?'

'I just do, okay? With plates and salt and pepper shakers and a silly little tablecloth to lay on the ground and sandwiches for the whole family...' Riley's voice trailed away. 'You ever had a picnic like that?'

Gil shook his head.

'Nor me,' Riley said.

No matter what Riley believed, Gil didn't think there was anything lucky about the next car that followed Junk into the rest stop. It was small and there were two people in the front, which meant there was double the chance of Riley being spotted. Even worse, the moment the woman in the passenger seat got out, she began waving her phone around, the torch jerking hither and thither.

'I'm going to get this all on film,' she cried in a shrill, excited voice.

Gil shrank deeper into the bushes. His mask of mud had dried so stiffly that his whole face ached.

'Aww, it's so cu—' The woman broke off as she caught her first real sight of Junk. She made a face. 'You sure that's a dog, Paulie? You sure it's not a coyote or something?'

'It's not a coyote!'

'Grab it. Not like that! Sneak up and *then* grab it.'

'I could use a hand here,' Paulie complained.

'I'm filming, aren't I?'

Riley was at the back of the car. Gil saw him raise the lid of the boot and peer inside, then bend forward for a closer look. *Perhaps there really is a picnic basket in there*, Gil thought. Something had certainly caught Riley's attention. He was leaning in so deeply that the whole of his upper body was inside the boot.

'We need to give it some food,' Gil heard the woman say. 'I'll go get that bag of crisps.' He saw the light on her phone suddenly sweeping towards the car.

There was no time to get away. Riley didn't even try. Instead, he plunged head-first into the boot, pulling the lid down after him in a single movement. Gil caught the click as it closed.

If the woman hadn't been so busy filming, she might have heard it too. But all her attention was fixed on trying to hold her phone steady as she groped for the crisps on the passenger seat.

'Salt and vinegar!' she announced, shaking the bag in front of the camera. 'Let's see if the doggie likes these...'

'What are you doing?' the man called. 'Stop wasting time!'

'*All right*, Paulie...'

Gil gazed anxiously at the boot, expecting Riley to emerge. Perhaps he hadn't heard the woman leave, he told himself, as time ticked by. Or perhaps... Gil tried to push the thought away. Riley *couldn't* be trapped. Cars had safety levers so that anyone locked in the boot would be able to open it from the inside. Any second now, Riley was going to jump out, grinning with triumph at his narrow escape.

What if this car didn't have a safety lever, though? Or the lever was jamme107d?

Riley had told Gil to stay in his hiding place on pain of death. Yet this was an emergency. Gil took a deep breath and crawled out of the bushes. He reached the rubbish bin and raised himself on to his heels, listening. By the sound of it, the man and woman were still busy trying to lure Junk into their clutches. Gil wondered how long the bag of crisps would last. Barely any time at all if Junk had anything to do with it.

The back of the car was about five metres away.

'Riley?' Gil whispered. A faint tapping sound came from the boot.

'*Riley?*' The tapping grew louder.

'Hang on,' Gil said. 'I'll get you out.' He crawled to the back of the car and raised his arm, searching for the boot release. Riley was tapping louder than ever.

'Be quiet, they'll *hear* you...' Gil grasped the boot release and rose to his feet to lift the lid.

'What are you doing?' the man said, looming out of the darkness.

Gil couldn't speak. 'Hey,' the man called over his shoulder, 'A kid's trying to break into our car!'

'I'm not,' Gil stuttered.

'What are you doing, then?'

The woman came up and shone her phone light on his face, blinding him.

'What are you doing?' the man repeated.

'I'm warning you, I'm recording this,' the woman said. 'I'm getting the whole thing on film.'

'I wasn't trying to break into the car,' Gil said, trying to shield his eyes. 'I was… looking for my dog.'

'Your dog?'

'You haven't seen him anywhere, have you?' Gil said.

Eighteen

Junk must have been enjoying the crisps. There was a hopeful look on his face as Gil and the others approached. He leered at them eagerly, his eyes blinking in the headlights, his body casting a long, nightmarish shadow over the ground.

'That's him,' Gil said. 'That's my dog!'

'We were going to rescue him,' the woman said, sounding indignant.

'There's something not right here,' the man said. 'What are you doing here by yourself at this time of night? Where do you live? And why is there mud on your face?'

'I fell,' Gil said, hastily wiping his cheek. He gestured vaguely in the direction of the trees. 'My house is really close. I guess I woke up, saw the dog was gone…'

'Why isn't he wearing a collar?'

'He slipped out of it,' Gil said. 'He's always doing that.'

'Why don't you put a harness on him, then?'

Gil didn't have a good answer for this. He patted Junk's bony head, trying to give himself time to think.

The woman turned off her phone and stuffed it in her pocket. 'Let's get out of here, Paulie.'

I have to keep them talking, Gil thought. He had to give Riley a chance to escape. 'He's a show dog, you know,' he said. 'He's won lots of prizes. They're very high-strung, show dogs. Easily spooked. Isn't that right, Junk?'

'What kind of show dog is called "Junk"?' the woman said with a smirk.

'That's his nickname. His show name is Sir Bedivere,' Gil said. 'Sir Bedivere Bollinger de la Pole.'

'The Third,' he added.

'Well, I've never seen anything like him,' the man said. 'What breed is he supposed to be?'

'He's a… a Saharan hunting dog. Trained to like, hunt for stuff. In the Sahara Desert.'

'For real?' the man said, in a tone of deep suspicion.

'I'm going to Google it,' the woman said, pulling out her phone again. 'How'd you spell "Saharan", Paulie?'

Gil felt the rise of panic. It was pointless to keep talking. Riley was well and truly locked in the boot. Even if he had all the time in the world, he still wouldn't be able to get out.

'I guess we ought to walk you back to your house,' the man was saying. 'It's not safe on your own out here.'

'It's okay,' Gil said hastily. 'It's only a few minutes away, I don't want to wake my parents…'

Riley might be stuck for hours. How long would it take for his air to run out? Better to be found now, anything was better than dying, and maybe, with surprise on his side, he'd have a chance of getting away…

It was almost too late. The couple had already returned to their car, they were opening the doors, getting inside.

'Hey,' Gil cried. 'I forgot to bring a leash, you don't have any rope, do you? In the boot of your car? Or string? Rope or string?'

The man shook his head. 'Don't keep anything like that in the boot.'

'Could you check? Could you open it and look?'

'Sorry,' the man said, buckling his seat belt. 'Get home safe now, okay?'

He shut the door and started the engine, lifting his hand in a brief wave as the car pulled out of the rest stop and on to the motorway. Gil heard it accelerate, as though making up for lost time, and then it was gone.

He stood in the silence, his hand on Junk's head and despair in his heart. Why had he babbled about rope and string? He should have told the truth. He should have shouted it at the top of his voice.

OPEN THE BOOT! THERE'S SOMEONE INSIDE!

He hadn't. He had just let them drive away.

'What am I going to do?' Gil pressed Junk tight to

his side, his eyes filling with tears. 'What am I going to *do*?'

An owl hooted and Junk bounded away. Gil looked up, saw the beam of a torch darting towards him through the trees.

'You saved my life, man,' Riley said.

Gil stared at him speechlessly, tears still running down his face. He knew Riley had seen them and would mock him for crying. But Riley didn't.

'I thought...' Gil gulped, fighting back a sob. 'I thought you were locked in.'

'I was. It was bad. Only got out by kicking the seat until it went forward. I crawled into the back of the car and escaped through a passenger door.'

Gil sniffed and wiped his wet, muddy face.

'I couldn't have done it if you hadn't kept them talking.' Riley rubbed his hand on his jeans and held it out for Gil to shake. 'We make a good team.'

The darkness was softening. It would be dawn soon. Riley and Gil lifted the cooler between them and jogged back to the island, Junk loping ahead. 'Sir Bedivere!' Riley kept saying. 'Sir Bedivere Bollinger, ha ha ha!'

It was the happiest Gil had ever felt in his life.

Nineteen

Life on the island settled into a rhythm. There were daily chores to be done. Tidying the camp, hunting for firewood, searching the perimeter for anything useful that might have been thrown from a passing car. If it had rained, they rinsed their clothes and cleaned themselves using a scrap of fabric for a washcloth and two cups of water – one to get wet and another to wash off the soap.

But these activities only took up a small part of each day. The rest of the time was spent in two ways. The first – and most important – revolved around food. Talking about food, looking for food, preparing food. The morning after Riley and Gil's adventure, they had risked a daytime fire and cooked the corn and the steaks, the smell almost too delicious to bear as they waited for the feast to be ready.

There were two ears of corn and a steak for each of them, including Junk. To begin with, they gobbled the food because they couldn't help themselves. Then they ate slowly, trying to make it last, until the sight of the nearly empty hubcap made them gobble again, fearful of missing out on the last scraps. When it was completely gone, they licked the hubcap clean and all their fingers one by one, and lay back, paralysed with contentment, their faces turned to the sky.

Yet all too soon they were hungry again. The blueberries were gone, and the peaches were not yet ripe, and there was never quite enough to eat. Gil had already lost so much weight that he had to keep his jeans up with a length of string.

When they weren't involved with issues relating to food, the boys were busy with the other main activity of the day, which was finding ways to entertain themselves. Riley had invented at least twenty games, from grass-flicking contests to snail races, but most of his time was spent training Junk to do tricks, each more outlandish than the one before. Junk could now play dead, walk on two legs for the length of the camp, and howl (or so Riley claimed, and Gil dared not contradict) to the tune of 'Twinkle Twinkle Little Star'.

Grayson was less active, partly to save energy – being twice as tall as the others, he was also twice as hungry – and partly because being bored didn't seem to worry him as much as it did his brother. He could pass a whole hour, sitting on his upturned tin, staring at the meadow and the trees beyond with a vacant look on his face. Then, as if responding to a signal that only he could hear, he would suddenly blink and shake his head and return to his whittling again.

'What are you making?' Gil asked, seeing him start work on a fresh stick.

'Teaspoon,' Grayson said.

'A *teaspoon*? Why are you making that?'

'Don't know,' Grayson mumbled, his head bent.

There was a long silence. 'My nan had a lot of teaspoons,' Grayson said finally, still not looking up. 'She kept them on a fancy shelf, all lined up. They had names on them – names of places. Sometimes pictures too, and sometimes they were in the shape of things, like a bell or a flower, or a castle. Whenever she went someplace new, my nan bought a teaspoon, and people got to know about it and started giving her teaspoons when *they* went someplace too.'

'I didn't know you had a nan,' Gil said.

'It was ages ago.' Grayson puffed his cheeks and blew a shaving off his stick. 'I used to visit her when I was little, and she always used to let me play with the spoons. I was the only one she allowed. She said she knew just by looking at me that I'd be careful with them.'

Gil watched him smooth the stick, the knife light in his hand. 'Is this the first teaspoon you've made?' he asked.

Grayson stood up without a word and went into the tent he shared with Riley. He returned with a roll of fabric. There were three small wooden spoons inside.

'You made these?' Gil cried. They were extraordinarily delicate, with slender, tapering stems.

At the top of each stem, Grayson had carved a different animal; a cricket, a frog, a crow – beautifully lifelike in every detail.

They were all creatures living on the island, Gil realised. Grayson hadn't been staring blankly into space for all those hours. He'd been *watching*.

'But they're not finished,' Gil said. The bowls of the spoons hadn't been shaped. They were still solid wooden ovals, as round as eggs.

'Can't do them with my knife,' Grayson admitted. 'Need something with a curved edge.'

Gil thought for a minute, then dug in his pocket for his penknife.

'Would this do?' he asked, pulling out one of the blades.

Grayson's face lit up. 'It would!'

'What animal are you going to carve on the next spoon?'

'You can choose, if you like,' Grayson said, still overcome with joy. 'Anything you want!'

'What about a fox? I saw one the other morning, only it was way too small to be a fox. Have *you* seen anything like that? It had weird blue eyes...'

Grayson shook his head.

'I probably just imagined it,' Gil said. 'You should carve Pez's condor instead. If she ever lets you see it.'

Twenty

Like the boys, Pez also had a daily routine, although hers was much stricter. She had to tend to her vegetables and look after the crickets and make sure that the bird didn't get too hungry, as well as cook her meals and sweep her camp with a broom she had made of dried rushes.

The bird only needed to be fed once or twice a week, which was lucky because it was hard work trekking up and down the motorway after dark, searching for the forlorn bodies of animals that had been killed by cars. Sometimes they were rabbits, sometimes possums, occasionally a raccoon. Recently they'd become more difficult to find and Pez suspected the boys' dog had begun competing with her in the search. She had seen him several times on the side of the road, a pale shape loping through the dark, following the scent of food.

Two days before, after a particularly long stretch between feedings, Pez had woken to find the bird gone. It was what she had wanted to happen, but instead of relief, a terrible, aching misery rose in her chest. Then she saw that he had only plodded a little way beyond the trees, his beak muddy as he searched for worms. That night she had found a dead turtle in the middle of the road, belly up in the bowl of its shell, and had hurried back to feed it to the bird.

Tomorrow, she told him silently. *You must leave tomorrow.*

Most of the roadkill Pez came across had been squashed – either entirely, or in part – under the wheels of the hurtling traffic. But some, flung clear of the road, was still intact. These she skinned before giving them to the bird, carefully cleaning each tiny pelt. When she had enough, she planned to stitch them together into a blanket for when the weather grew cold.

The boys would be gone by then. Their supplies couldn't last much longer, even with the extra food they managed to steal. Pez was astonished by their ignorance. Apart from strawberries and blueberries, they didn't seem to know that there were edible plants in abundance on the island. They were so clueless that they didn't collect snails to eat, they played with them instead. Pez wouldn't have believed it if she hadn't seen it with her own eyes. The boys crouched over racetracks made of sticks, cheering and bickering at the tops of their voices. *Mine's in the lead! That's not yours! Yours is going backwards!*

When their food runs out, they'll have to go back to where they came from, Pez thought. She would have the place to herself again.

She fetched her slingshot from the hollow tree, fitted a pebble, and fired it at a tin tied to a distant branch. She heard the high, musical *ping* as it hit, her hands already placing another pebble in the sling. Daily target practice had perfected her aim, and now she rarely missed, even when the sun dazzled her eyes, or the tin swayed in the breeze.

She would have the place to herself. She wouldn't have to hear the boys calling to each other, their whoops as they ran in the rain, pulling their T-shirts off and waving them in the air, their chatter around the fire every night. She wouldn't have to watch Gil approach her camp, as he had done every morning for the last three days, calling out, 'Hello? Hello?' in a hopeful voice, even though she kept on ignoring him.

Pez had placed the bottle in the shape of the Eiffel Tower on a flat stone in the tepee where she slept. She had made the tepee out of tightly woven sticks and moss, with a tarpaulin canopy to shelter it from the rain. It was so cramped inside that when Pez was lying down, the stone and bottle took up the rest of the space, and when she woke in the morning, it was the first thing she saw.

The bottle was the most precious thing that Pez had ever been given. The Starborn didn't approve of gifts unless they were items of use. A cooking pot, for example. Or a pair of hand-knitted socks. Every weekend during the summer, they drove to the nearest town and sold the vegetables they'd grown, although they never made a lot of money. Just enough to buy the basic things they needed, and they didn't need much.

They lived simply, camping in the fields around the farm, and taking it in turns to sleep in the barn when the weather was cold. Only Juno Ray and her two favourite assistants lived in the farmhouse. The farmhouse had comfy sofas and hot running water and a clock that chimed the hour. *It had nothing*, Pez thought, *as rich and rare as the bottle in the shape of the Eiffel Tower.*

Pez knew she couldn't bear to give the bottle back, but keeping it felt impossible. Gil had given it to her because he wanted to be her friend. If she kept it, he might think he'd succeeded. And Pez didn't want to be friends. Not with Gil, not with anyone.

It would be better if she could think of the bottle as a bartering item rather than a gift. Gil had said it was a thank you for helping him get better, but Pez knew it was a far from equal exchange. Anyone could make a potion and once used, it was gone. She needed to give him something else. It was the only way they could ever be even.

She spent a whole morning deciding what to do. Then she went to the pond and cut a dozen of the tallest rushes. After she had laid them to dry in the sun for a day, she soaked them overnight in a tub of water. In the morning, she rolled the rushes back and forth beneath a stone until they were as soft and flexible as leather. She selected the best and began to braid them.

The braiding took a long time. Pez wanted it to be as strong and as neat as possible. When she was finally done, she made a loop at one end of the braid and attached an acorn to the other end, to serve as a toggle.

Gil had come to see her for three days in a row, without any success. Pez told herself that he'd probably given up by now, and she didn't care if he had, not even slightly. But on the fourth morning, she was up in the tree watching, the rush braid coiled tight in her hand.

She saw him cross the meadow and stop.

'Hello?' he called.

Pez swung down from her perch, landing silent and unseen. She hesitated, then walked into the meadow, counting each step until she was exactly halfway between Gil and the sheltering trees. She placed the braid on the ground and backed away, her heart hammering.

'What is it?' Gil uncoiled the braid slowly. 'Why is there an acorn at one end?'

Pez made a circle with her thumb and forefinger. He frowned, not understanding. She raised her hand and pressed the circle against her eye.

'My hagstone?' Gil said. 'How do you know about that?' He glanced at the braid again. 'It's so I can hang it around my neck, isn't it?' He fished in his pocket for the pebble, and she watched him thread it on to the braid and fasten the acorn toggle.

'Now I'll always know where it is,' Gil said, pressing the pebble against his chest. 'It'll always be safe.'

Pez gazed at his pleased face with a feeling of relief. She didn't have to be friends with him now. They were even.

Twenty-one

'We have to get that girl on our side,' Grayson announced that evening as they sat around the fire. 'She knows how to do things.'

'She knows how to do *everything*,' Gil said.

'I wonder where she learned it all,' Grayson said. 'I mean, where would you have to come from to learn stuff like that?'

'Somewhere strange,' Riley said. 'It's like she was being raised to get ready for the Zombie Apocalypse or something.'

'That's only in movies,' Gil said, although he had to admit he couldn't think of any other explanation for Pez's extraordinary survival skills.

'Well, wherever it was, it must have been bad,' Riley said. 'Bad enough to make her stop talking.'

'Maybe she *can't* talk,' Grayson suggested. 'You know, born like that...'

'Or maybe she just doesn't want to,' Gil said. 'She doesn't like people much. After she gave me the braid, I asked if Grayson could come and see the condor, and she shook her head and ran off.'

'We need her help,' Grayson said. 'If we don't get it, we'll run out of food and we'll have to leave.'

'We don't need her help!' Riley cried. 'We've still got plenty of things to eat, and I steal stuff, don't I?'

'I don't want to leave,' Gil said softly. 'I like it here. I don't have anywhere else to go.'

'Nor do we,' Grayson said.

'We have loads of places to go,' Riley protested. 'We can go *anywhere*!'

There was a long silence. Riley picked up a stick and stabbed at the fire until the air was furious with sparks. 'Okay, *okay*!' he muttered. 'Maybe we do need her. But she's never going to help us, not in a million years.'

Gil thought. 'She likes gifts,' he said. 'You should give her something. Something really nice.'

It was past noon the following day, and Pez hadn't finished even half of her chores. She was too troubled and distracted. She'd tried target practice for a while, but after missing the tin five times in a row, she had flung her slingshot down in frustration. Now she sat with her chin on her knees, angrily scraping the earth with a twig, her mind far away.

It wasn't right, what the boys had done. It wasn't fair.

She'd made things even with Gil, but they'd ruined it. And Pez had no idea how to put things right again. All she knew was that it was going to take more – a lot more – than a crumby little rush braid.

Gil had appeared in his usual spot that morning, and at first it didn't look as if he was carrying anything. Then he'd reached into his pocket and brought out a tiny package.

'It's for you.' He placed it on the ground. 'From Riley and Grayson.'

Pez didn't take the package. She didn't even glance at it. She clenched her fists and stared at Gil with stony, unblinking eyes until he turned and went away. Even then, she'd waited, counting in her head for three whole minutes before going to see what he'd left. She wouldn't pick it up, she told herself. She would just *look*.

It was something wrapped in a dock leaf, tied with a length of dental floss. Pez dropped to her heels and examined the knot. *If I can undo it*, she thought, *I can find out what's inside and tie it up again without anyone knowing*. She rested the package on her knee and picked at it carefully, frowning in concentration. But the knot was too small and tight, even for her nimble fingers.

She would have to slide the floss off. No more than a corner, enough for her to take a quick peek. The dock leaf had ideas of its own. It sprang open before she could stop it.

Pez almost stopped breathing when she saw what lay inside. It was a gold earring. Not plastic or tin, but actual gold. She knew it was real by the shine of it, and the weight when she picked it up. How heavy it felt in the palm of her hand, how mysteriously *right*. As if it had always belonged there. Desolation filled her heart. She couldn't keep it. She had to give it back.

But.

If she gave it back, she would have to wrap it up again, and she couldn't because the dental floss was tangled up. They'd know for sure she'd opened it. What if they thought she'd returned their gift because she didn't like it? Or because it wasn't good enough? If that happened, they might try to give her something better, something so valuable that no matter how long she lived, she'd never get even.

She couldn't give the earring back, Pez decided. She *had* to keep it.

And that meant she had work to do.

Grayson had been right when he'd told Gil that it was hard to hear Pez coming. There was no telling how long she'd been standing there, in the shadow of the blue tent, before Riley happened to glance in her direction.

It was almost dark. Grayson had lit the fire and decided what they would eat as he always did, just as

Riley always prepared the food and made sure that nobody took more than their share. That left Gil to do the cleaning up, which was the easiest job of all, since Junk's tongue did most of the work.

There were beans for supper that night, and Riley was busy slicing the last two mozzarella sticks to add to the pan when he looked up and saw Pez.

'What's the matter?' Grayson said.

Riley jerked his head in the direction of the blue tent, his eyes wide.

Away from the safety of her own camp, Pez looked even more scrawny than ever, and ten times as fierce. She glared at the boys as if daring them to move, or even breath too loud, then stepped warily forward. Without shifting her gaze for even a fraction of a second, she reached into a cloth bag slung across her body and placed three objects by the fire.

Riley made a noise as if he was trying to speak and swallow at the same time. He made it again.

'Are those... *potatoes*?' he finally croaked.

Pez had already gone.

The next night she brought a bunch of wild garlic and a carrot. The night after that, a bundle of nettles that must have cost her an hour and many stings to gather. After she laid them down, she pointed at the boys' cooking pan, and then at the water barrels, indicating that the nettles needed to be boiled before being eaten. Then she vanished, before they had time to thank her.

They tried being silent, they tried speaking kindly.

But nothing could make her stay longer than she had to, or soften – even for an instant – the wild, warning look in her eyes.

It took an accident on the motorway for that to happen.

Twenty-two

Whenever he was alone, either on his way to the bathroom hole at the far end of the island, or early in the morning before the others were awake, Gil kept a lookout for the fox. The more he thought about the creature he'd seen nosing in the remains of the fire, the more convinced he became that he hadn't been mistaken. He'd seen a fox; he was sure of it. Then he remembered the animal's strange blue eyes and he was filled with doubt once more.

His chances of spotting it again were slim as he was practically never alone. Junk was never far away, or Grayson crashing though bushes as he collected kindling, or Riley fooling around with the latest thing to catch his attention. On the morning of the accident, Riley was amusing himself with the contents of a stolen toiletries bag, using his brother as a model. Grayson sat with a patient look on his face as Riley placed a dozen Velcro curlers in his hair.

'Interesting,' Riley said, pausing to admire the effect. 'Now for the lipstick...'

He was interrupted by a shriek; the anguished sound a car makes when it brakes too hard, too suddenly and too late. Riley's hand jerked, sending a trail of red from Grayson's mouth all the way up to his ear.

There was a loud bang, and then – softer yet far more ominous – a crunching noise that seemed to go on for a long time, although it lasted only an instant.

Riley sprang to his feet and raced towards the trees that screened the road. Two minutes later he was back, panting almost too much to speak.

'Accident,' he gasped. 'Here, right here, on the verge... a van and a car with its front smashed, totally *crushed*. It must have gone into the back of the van... bunch of people inside.'

'Are they okay?' Gil said, 'Are they dead?'

'I don't know. But, yeah, probably.'

'We ought to go look,' Grayson said. 'Maybe we could help.'

'Not if they're dead!' Riley cried. 'We can't help them if they're *dead*!'

'They might not be,' Gil protested.

'We ought to try at least,' Grayson agreed.

As they stood in panicky indecision, they heard the thin cry of a siren.

'See? They don't need our help,' Riley said. 'There's an ambulance coming. Police too, I bet. In less than a minute, there's gonna be fifty people here.'

There was no need for the emergency signal. All

three boys turned at once and raced to dismantle the camp. They had practised the routine over and over, but it was different this time. *It doesn't feel like a game*, Gil thought, feverishly shoving possessions into his backpack. Over his head, Riley and Grayson were already tugging down his tent, buckling poles and tripping over ropes in their haste. Gil flung his backpack into the nearest bush and rushed to help the others drag the tarpaulin over their possessions and the stolen luggage. But now that the risk was real, he could see it wasn't much of a disguise, even after they covered the tarp with a scattering of brush and dried leaves.

It might fool someone at first glance. It wouldn't if they looked again.

The siren had grown louder with each passing second. It was a shriek now, and a second had joined it, still distant but approaching even more rapidly than the first. Riley threw the tin-can stools among the grass, Grayson pulled down the washing line, and Gil kicked earth into the ashes of the fire.

'It's good enough,' Riley cried. 'It has to be!'

They darted towards their hiding places; Riley and Gil flat on their stomachs in two different parts of the meadow, Grayson – too big to disappear among even the tallest of grass – at the top of the lookout tree, safely screened by branches. Junk had already taken cover. He lay in a dip among the blueberry bushes, his snout between his paws, his body as flat as a stain on the ground.

Gil wasn't sure when the siren abruptly cut off. He was only aware of the appalling silence that followed, and the judder of the earth as it beat against his heart. He heard voices beyond the trees, the crackle of radio static, and the sound of someone crying. *Not a grown-up*, Gil thought. *Only little kids wail like that.*

He wondered where Pez was. She wouldn't have wasted time panicking as they had done. She would have vanished the minute she heard the collision, hiding where nobody would find her, even if they tramped over every inch of the island.

Why hadn't he and Riley planned better hiding places? Grayson was difficult to spot up in his tree, but they were simply lying in the meadow. Anyone venturing through the trees to explore what lay beyond would have to be half-blind not to notice the trails of flattened grass and the garish green flash of Riley's bandana.

But they wouldn't venture through the trees, Gil told himself. The people were not there to explore. They wouldn't see anything for the same reason passing cars never saw anything. Because they wouldn't be looking. It was just another green patch on the motorway. Nowhere Island; neither one place nor another, but only and for ever in-between.

Gil rested his head on his hands to shield it from the prickly grass and closed his eyes. The people would leave. The ambulance would drive away. All they had to do was wait.

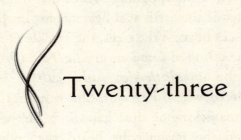

Twenty-three

Gil didn't have a watch. A few years ago, one of his foster parents had given him an old one, but he had left it behind, either at his next foster home, or the one after that. So he had no way of knowing how long he lay there, waiting for the coast to clear. It might have been half an hour, although he guessed it was probably closer to forty-five minutes. Long enough for both of Grayson's legs to go to sleep. Gil raised his head, craning his neck towards the lookout tree. But he was too low to the ground to see more than halfway up the trunk.

There was a rustle in the grass, and Riley was suddenly in front of him.

'What are you *doing*? We're not meant to—'

'Never heard me coming, did you?' Riley's voice was hoarse with triumph. His bandana had slipped down his forehead almost covering his eyes.

'I think they've gone.'

'How d'you know?'

'Haven't heard anything for ages.'

They cocked their heads, listening.

'Ambulance is definitely gone,' Riley said. 'I heard it.'

'No siren, though,' he added.

'That means nobody was hurt, right? They'd have used the siren if anyone was hurt.'

'How do I know?' Riley said.

It was almost noon, the sun fierce on the back of Gil's neck, his skin alive with the feathery creep of marching insects.

'We should go look,' Riley said.

'What was that?'

'What was what?'

'I thought I heard voices,' Gil said.

'We'll sneak up, then. Just in case. But we gotta stay low.' Riley bent his arms and made a rowing motion, chin down and elbows out. 'Commando style!'

Gil wanted to laugh but Riley was giving him the death stare, his eyes boring through the folds of his bandana.

'Ready?' Riley hissed. Gil nodded.

'Okay, then. Follow me.' Riley swivelled and moved off. 'See how I'm leading with my knees?' he said, looking back. 'It's all in the knees. Like climbing up a cliff only it's flat.'

'I think it's called "the ground",' Gil was tempted to say, although he didn't.

They inched their way to the edge of the meadow and were about to rise to their heels when a voice on the other side of the trees stopped them.

'I'm *bored*. When can we go?' The voice was high-pitched, hovering on the brink of a whine. *A kid*, Gil thought. Probably the one he'd heard crying before.

'We have to wait for the pick-up truck, honey,' a woman said. 'It won't be long.'

'That's what you said five hours ago!'

The boys stared at each other. Riley made a fork with two fingers, pointed at his eyes and then in the direction of the voices. Gil nodded and crouching they crept forward, moving from tree to tree. They dropped to their knees and crawled into the bushes on the edge of the grassy verge. The accident had happened at a spot where the motorway dipped briefly, giving the boys a good view from their vantage above.

Riley had been right. The car was a wreck, the bonnet crumpled like a stomped-on tin can. Tiny bits of glass from the shattered windscreen lay all around, sparkling as they caught the sun. It was hard to imagine how anyone could have survived such a crash, but they had. They were sitting in a pocket of shade not far away, a scruffy overheated-looking dog flopped on the grass beside them.

'Not a scratch,' Riley whispered in Gil's ear. 'Airbags must've saved them.'

There were four people. A mum and dad, and two boys, one about five years old, the other closer to eight. Even though they didn't really look the same, Gil knew they were a family because they were all versions of each other. As if they'd been drawn from the same description by four different artists.

'Are you *sure* the pick-up truck is coming?' the younger of the boys said. 'What if it doesn't see us and drives right by?'

'It won't do that, Ashton,' his father said. He was sitting with his arms resting easily on his knees, his face calm. 'I'm watching for it.'

'Our car will get fixed, won't it?'

His father hesitated. 'Well, I'm not sure about that. But we'll figure something out.'

'The important thing is that we're all okay,' the mum said. 'That's the important thing.' She smiled, although Gil could tell it wasn't a real smile. It was too sudden and too bright. As if she was trying not to cry.

'Can I play with my drone?' the older boy asked.

'Not a good idea, Troy,' his father told him. 'Too dangerous this close to the motorway.'

'But I won't fly it over the motorway!'

'I said no, okay?'

'That old pick-up truck better come soon,' Ashton interrupted. ''Cos I really need to use the bathroom.'

His mother smiled, this time for real. 'You don't have to wait, honey. Go over there a little way. It's fine, we won't look.'

'Promise?'

'Like we *want* to watch you going pee-pee,' his brother said, pulling a disgusted face.

The little boy stood up and began jiggling from foot to foot, staring at the passing cars. '*They'll* see me... I have to find someplace in the bushes.'

Gil and Riley froze. He was looking right in their direction. Then his eyes moved on, still searching.

'Don't go far,' his mother said. 'I want you back in two minutes, you hear?'

He nodded and the boys saw him trot away, heading towards an opening in the trees. It was the same opening that Gil had taken, the night he'd chased Riley on to the island and run smack into the trunk of the lookout tree.

Gil felt Riley's fingers digging into his arm, although neither of them spoke. They didn't need to because they were both thinking the same thing.

What if that kid sees Grayson?

Twenty-four

Although he was too high up to hear any conversation, Grayson had a clear view of the grassy verge from his spot in the lookout tree, along with a stretch of motorway on either side. Unlike the others, he had seen everything that had happened after the ambulance and the police arrived. For a while, everyone had rushed around, getting things out of the ambulance, and putting them back again, talking on their phones and talking to each other. Then they had gone, leaving the family sitting on the ground next to the wreck of their car.

Grayson had watched them for a bit, but his attention had soon drifted to a hawk, circling high above him. Three or four smaller birds had surrounded the hawk, darting and swerving across its flight path, as if trying to drive it away. But away from what? Grayson scanned the empty sky, his thoughts moving from one distant cloud to the next, as wordless as the breeze.

He started suddenly and glanced down. Nothing had changed. The family were still sitting there. Grayson shifted uncomfortably on his branch. Like Ashton, he needed to pee. The feeling had come over him with great urgency as it often did. Not because he had no warning signs, but because he was usually too busy thinking about something else to pay any attention until it was almost too late. He took another quick look at the family, then twisted his body and swung from his perch, his feet reaching for the branch below.

If Grayson had waited thirty seconds longer, he would have seen Ashton get up and start heading his way. And if he hadn't been rushing to get to the bottom of the tree, he might have spotted the little boy, approaching through the green gloom. But Grayson's attention was fixed on where he was placing his hands and feet. He reached the last branch, dangled, then dropped.

Ashton was standing in front of him, barely two metres away.

They stared at each other in shock. Grayson had lost two of his curlers in his dash up the tree, but the rest were still in place, along with an assortment of leaves and two large twigs, stuck fast in the Velcro. Riley's lipstick was also still in place, stretching like a huge, red, horribly lopsided grin from ear to chin.

Ashton's mouth opened and his eyes filled with terror.

He's going to scream, Grayson thought. *The minute he catches his breath, he's going to scream louder than anyone has ever screamed before.*

Grayson's first instinct was to run, although he knew it would be pointless. The little boy had seen him, and as soon as he raised the alarm, Grayson would be followed. Equally it was useless to stay where he was, rooted to the spot in panic. Out of sheer desperation, he did the first thing that came into his head.

He began to dance.

His movements were timid to begin with. He swayed, arms waving, shifting his weight slowly from foot to foot, his gaze fixed earnestly ahead.

He's going to scream. Any second now...

Ashton was still staring at him open-mouthed, but it was now more a gape of astonishment than of fear. As if he couldn't believe his eyes. Encouraged, Grayson tried a couple of skips. He raised his arms and barrelled them, plunged to the left, then to the right, his dusty shoes thudding against the ground. He was about to risk a full twirl when the little boy turned and bolted back the way he'd come.

From their shelter in the bushes, Gil and Riley saw Ashton burst from the trees and race across the grass to his parents.

'Uh oh,' Riley muttered. 'Don't like the look of this.'

Ashton was trying to say something, but he was panting too frantically to get the words out. 'What is it, honey?' his mum said. 'What's wrong?'

'There's someone there,' Ashton babbled, pointing wildly behind him.

His parents stood up, gazing warily towards the trees. 'Who was it?' the man said. 'What did you see?'

'A giant!' Ashton squeaked. 'A giant troll clown thing! It landed right in front of me out of nowhere!'

'Cool!' his brother said.

'It had big fat curlers in its hair,' Ashton said, clearly beginning to enjoy himself. His parents glanced at each other.

'You sure you didn't imagine it?' his mum asked. 'You know how good you are at imagining things.'

'Like when you said there was a goblin in the pantry and it was only a sack of potatoes,' his brother added.

'It *was* a goberlin!'

'Never mind that now,' his dad interrupted hastily. 'This giant troll thing. What did it do when it saw you?'

'It started to dance.' Ashton grinned. 'It's a *really* bad dancer.'

'I see…' His parents exchanged another look, smiling at each other. Then they sat down again.

'Aren't you even going to look for it?' Ashton protested.

'I'm guessing it's vanished already,' his mum said, patting the ground next to her. 'Sit here with me. The pick-up truck will be arriving any minute now.'

'But I *saw* it!'

'Maybe you did, but it must be long gone.' She smoothed his hair fondly. 'I bet it was even more scared to see you than you were to see it.'

Riley leaned towards Gil. 'She's got that right!' he whispered, sounding gleeful.

'They nearly believed him,' Gil said, his heart still hammering. 'What if they decide to look, just to make sure?'

'Nah, we're safe.'

'We ought to go find Grayson.'

'Yeah,' Riley said, not moving. He was staring at the family on the grass verge. The mum, the dad, the two kids. The little dog fast asleep, nose twitching as it dreamed.

There was a strange expression on Riley's face. Gil had seen it before. It had been the night they stole the steaks, when they'd been lying on the side of the road, waiting for another car to rob, and Riley had said he was on a lucky streak. The look on his face as he stared at the family was the same as when he'd described the picnic hamper he was hoping to find.

Like someone on a dark street, who stops for a moment to gaze through a window at the warm, friendly light inside.

Twenty-five

Grayson was back at the dismantled camp, trying – unsuccessfully – to stay out of sight. He had removed the curlers and his hair was a mass of dusty, haphazard ringlets that bounced like springs whenever he moved his head.

'There he is,' Riley cried. 'The giant troll clown himself!'

'What did you call me?'

'It's what the kid thought you were. A giant troll clown. Also, a rubbish dancer.'

Grayson's cheeks, pink with lipstick, grew pinker still. 'Yeah,' he mumbled. 'I don't know what made me do that...'

'It was fire!' Riley said. 'A stroke of genius!'

'Are they gone?'

'No, but they soon will be. I think we're safe. We'll wait a bit and then get the camp sorted out, right, Gil?'

Gil nodded, although he was only half-listening. He was suddenly aware of the noise of insects, or rather of one insect, louder than all the rest. It was a wasp, he guessed, although it must be huge. In the time it took for this to pass through his mind, the noise had grown so much louder that Gil knew it couldn't be a wasp – or any sort of insect.

He looked up, saw nothing, turned to look behind him.

'Get down!' Riley shrilled, violently yanking Gil's arm.

The three boys flung themselves flat in the grass as a dark shape rose above the trees. Troy had been told not to play with his drone, but he must have decided that catching sight of a dancing, giant troll clown was worth getting into trouble for.

'It's coming nearer,' Gil gasped.

'There's no way it won't see us,' Grayson said. 'It might have seen us already.'

'We're finished,' Riley said. 'It's filming everything and there's nothing—'

He broke off. Pez was racing towards them across the meadow, a blur of skinny brown limbs and flying hair, reaching for something as she ran. Without slowing, or even breaking her stride, her arm stretched back. She aimed.

The pebble hit the drone with a sharp bang, sending it hurtling off course, parts flying in all directions. Pez was already fitting another pebble in her sling, but there was no need for a second shot. The drone – what was left of it – tried to right itself, gave a last feeble buzz, and fell like a stone into a patch of nettles.

Immediately, Junk shot out of his hiding place and tore after it. He retrieved it and deposited his prize at Riley's feet, his tail wagging with such triumph that his scrawny haunches shook. But for once, Riley paid him no attention. He was too busy staring at Pez. All of them were.

She stood, shoulders tensed, her sling still raised, pebble at the ready.

'That,' Riley said, his voice shrivelled to a rasp by awe, 'is the baddest-ass thing. I. Have. Ever. Seen.'

Grayson nodded in heartfelt agreement, his curls bobbing. 'Ever, ever,' he echoed, temporarily unable to come up with any other word. 'Ever, ever, *ever*.'

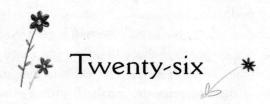

Twenty-six

Pez had planned to bring the boys a freshly killed rabbit that night. But the whole time she was skinning it, she was aware of the bird hunched nearby, carefully not looking at her.

I'm not giving it to you, Pez said in her mind to the bird.

A delicate pink flush spread over the bird's naked head, as if he was mortified by the mere suggestion. Pez removed the last of the skin, then gutted the rabbit swiftly and neatly and placed it on a large leaf.

Stop not looking at me, Pez told the bird.

The bird hesitated, as if he had been about to take a tiny step forward but had changed his mind at the last minute. Instead, he tried a more subtle approach. As Pez busied herself making a tidy package of the leaf-wrapped meat, he shifted his weight and began to lean. Slowly, casually, inch by inch, his gaze fixed innocently on a random spot in the middle distance.

Pez sat back on her heels and stared at him. If he leaned any closer, he would topple over. She sighed, unwrapped the rabbit and placed it between the bird's knobby talons.

After this, you've got to pull yourself together, she said silently. *You've got to fly back to where you came from.*

Since she couldn't bring the rabbit, Pez decided to make a dish of crickets, mashed with a couple of potatoes and a handful of wild basil. It was dark when she arrived at the boys' camp, the fire already well established. Normally by this time, the boys would be sitting around the flames, watching in silent fascination as their food cooked. But tonight, they were simply standing there, as though waiting for something.

'There you are!' Gil said.

'We got you a chair,' Grayson said, gesturing towards a fourth tin can.

'You saved us!' Riley cried.

Pez shook her head. She hadn't done it for them. She'd only been thinking of saving herself. Well, that was *mostly* what she'd been thinking. But if they believed she'd done it for them – even partly – then they'd assume... Pez's heart thumped in alarm... they'd assume she *wanted* them to be on the island. Eating the fruit and making a mess and putting them all in danger by stealing from cars.

'Where'd you learn to shoot like that?' Riley asked. 'That was, like, top-level *sniper*.'

'We thought maybe you'd sit with us,' Gil said. 'Just for a bit.'

Pez didn't want to sit with them. If she did, she might start to like them, and she couldn't risk that happening. But there was something about the way they were looking at her – with such admiration in their eyes – that made her hesitate.

Pez wasn't used to being in the spotlight. Among the Starborn, children were discouraged from drawing attention to themselves. It was called 'showing off'. When Pez noticed, for example, that their scarecrow wasn't keeping the birds away, and suggested they make another with a head that twirled around in the wind, that was 'showing off'. When she sold more vegetables in town than anyone else, that was 'showing off' too. Showing off was bad. But 'trying to be clever' was even worse.

Trying to be clever was different from trying to be helpful or trying to be kind. It wasn't a good thing. Whenever anyone told Pez she was trying to be clever, it made her feel ashamed. They mostly said it when she asked questions. Pez had been full of questions when she was small. '*When we go back to the stars will we still need to use the bathroom?*' she had asked. '*Can we take the chickens with us? What about the goat? Are there other goats up there? Will it be lonely all by itself?*'

Juno Ray stared at her with her sharp little eyes. 'Stop trying to be clever, dear,' she said. 'Nobody likes a smarty pants.'

'I know you don't mean to cause trouble,' Pez's mum said. 'But I wish you would *try* to fit in and not ask so many questions. You need to trust Juno Ray. Not just for your own sake, but for ours too. Do you understand how important that is?'

Pez didn't, but seeing the worried look on her mum's face, she decided to keep quiet. She nodded and her mum held her tight and told her she loved her.

After that, Pez stopped asking questions. She tried to fit in. She *trusted*.

'You saved us!' Riley cried again. 'I don't know how you made that shot.'

Pez wasn't sure how she'd made it either. She had never been proud of herself before and she liked how it felt, how it filled her chest and held her, calm and steady. She wouldn't sit with them, she decided. But perhaps she would sit *by* them, keeping a safe distance.

Pez placed the plate of cricket mash next to the fire, then made a wide circle and sat down, her legs crossed and her back straight. The boys looked at each other and then, to her relief, took their places without further comment.

'Is this what I think it is?' Riley said, peering warily at the cricket mash.

There was an awkward silence.

'Perhaps if we heated it up...' Grayson ventured. He tipped the mash into a pan, holding it at arm's length as if it might explode at any second, then set the pan on the fire.

Riley was the first to dip his fork and take a tiny mouthful. Pez noticed the gold hoop in his ear. She'd considered wearing hers too, as a necklace, perhaps, or woven into a reed bracelet. But it still felt too precious for that. She had placed it in her tepee, next to the bottle in the shape of the Eiffel Tower, on a bed of moss as rich and velvety as the inside of a jewel box.

'It's not too bad,' Riley said, taking another – larger – forkful.

'I card taste anyding,' Grayson said.

'Nor cab I,' Gil muttered.

'Stop holding your breath,' Riley ordered. 'It's quite good. Sort of nutty.'

Pez watched them eat, sharing the food between them. They didn't offer her any, or even look at her. *They're pretending to ignore me*, Pez thought. As if she was some rare, wild animal who might be spooked by the smallest hint of attention.

'What story are you going to tell tonight?' Grayson asked, after the meal was over.

'I don't know,' Gil said. 'I haven't decided.'

'Tell us about that family,' Riley said. 'Like, what they're doing now, and what happened with their car.'

Gil thought for a moment or two.

'They're staying at a motel, all of them in one room.'

'Why didn't they get two rooms?'

'Because they can't afford to. The mum and the kids and the little dog are on the bed, and the dad is sleeping on the sofa. He's too tall to fit on it and the sofa cover is kind of greasy, but he keeps saying how comfortable he is, so the mum doesn't feel guilty for being on the bed.'

'What a sucker,' Riley said.

'The kids are asleep,' Gil continued. 'But the mum and dad are too sad and worried to sleep. In the morning, they're going to have to tell the kids that their trip to Disney World isn't going to happen. They've been saving for years for this trip, thinking about it, planning every detail. But now they're going to have to use the money they saved on fixing the car, although it's so smashed up they'll probably have to buy a new one.

'So, they're in the motel room, and the mum is sort of lying there, staring at the ceiling, fingering her necklace, trying to figure out what to do. And then she gets an idea.'

Gil paused. 'Did you see that necklace she was wearing?'

The boys shook their heads. They had been pretending to ignore her before, now they were so engrossed in the story that they'd completely forgotten Pez was there.

'I'm surprised you didn't notice that necklace,' Gil said. 'It was a blue stone on a gold chain, and it really, really sparkled when it caught the light. That's because it's a sapphire, a real one. The mum inherited it from her grandma, and it's worth a ton of money.'

'How did the grandma get it?' Riley wanted to know. 'She was a jewel smuggler, wasn't she?'

'The mum knows she shouldn't wear the necklace all the time because it's so valuable,' Gil went on, ignoring the interruption. 'But she's always thought, what's the point of having something beautiful if you can't enjoy it? Then, as she's lying there, she gets an idea. What's the point of having something valuable if you can't sell it? So that's what she decides she's going to do. First thing in the morning, she's going to find a place to pawn the necklace, even though she knows she'll only get about half of what it's worth.'

'She's going to sell it?' Riley blurted out. 'Just so she can go to Disney World? That doesn't make sense.'

'No sense at all,' Grayson agreed.

'She's not going to sell it so she can go to Disney World!' Gil cried. 'You're missing the point. She's going to sell it so the kids won't be disappointed.'

Grayson let out a long breath. 'Ohhhh.'

There was silence. Even Riley seemed stunned.

'The kids are still in trouble, though,' he said, trying to rally. 'They were told not to fly that drone. It must've cost a *lot* and they're going to be really punished for losing it.'

'They won't get punished because it did cost a lot,' Gil said. 'Their dad told them that losing it was punishment enough.'

Riley shook his head, defeated. 'Now I *know* you're making this whole thing up,' he said.

Twenty-seven

It was the height of summer. The grass was at its tallest, and the leaves were at their greenest, and the flowers in the meadow burned with colour as though lit from within. The air was still, too warped by heat to stir, and even the sun seemed motionless, a burning nail hammered into the flat blue wall of the sky.

It hadn't rained for a week and the boys' supply of water was running low. Every day, Gil had to reach his cup deeper into the fast-emptying barrels.

'It's a pity we don't have any rum,' Riley said. 'That's what pirates drank when their water ran out. They chugged it by the gallon.'

''Least we've got plenty of peaches,' Grayson said, taking a huge bite out of the peach he was holding. He wiped the juice off his sweaty face and took another bite. 'We've got so many, we'll never be able to eat them all.'

'Pez is drying them,' Gil said. 'She's got them cut into slices laid in the sun. She's storing them for winter.'

'Why didn't we think of that?' Riley said.

Since the night of the accident, Pez had joined the boys around the fire every evening. She had kept her distance at first, but each time she had crept a little closer, until one night she was sitting so close that as the hubcap of food made its round, it felt natural to hand it to her too. She stiffened for a second, then selected a tiny scrap and passed the hubcap on.

Next day, she allowed Grayson into her camp to see the condor. When he caught sight of the bird, perched in its usual spot beside the hollow tree, his face lost all expression, wiped clean by wonder.

'I think it can fly,' Gil said. 'But it doesn't seem to want to.'

There was a long silence, as though Grayson had forgotten how to speak. 'It's waiting,' he said at last.

'For what?'

'I don't know.'

Grayson sat by the condor for a while, his chin resting on his vast, bony knees. *They could be twins*, Gil thought, smiling to himself. That evening, Grayson started whittling a new teaspoon, working on it late into the night, until the last gleam had left the fire and darkness forced him to bed.

Although Pez shared their evening meals and allowed them to visit, and smiled from time to time when nobody was looking, she still refused to speak. Even to Gil.

She was teaching him how to use her slingshot, although after an hour of trying, he hadn't even come close to hitting the tin target.

'It's hopeless,' he said, as Pez patiently handed him another pebble. 'I can't concentrate. It's just too hot.'

'I like your headband,' he said. She had fastened her gold earring to a thin strip of leather and tied it around her brow. It brought out the gold of her skin and the darker, liquid gold of her hair.

'What will happen to your vegetables if it doesn't rain soon?' he asked. 'How long can they last?' He looked up at the burning blue sky. 'I saw a fox the other day, only it was too small to be a fox and its eyes were a weird colour. Do you think I imagined it? Have you seen it too?'

Pez began gathering the scattered pebbles, not looking at him.

'I don't know why I keep asking you questions,' Gil said. 'You're never going to answer, are you?'

There was something special for supper that evening. The night before, while Gil cowered in his usual spot in the bushes, Riley had swiped a large cardboard box from the back of a van. Inside was the biggest cake either of them had ever seen. Before they found the cake, something odd happened. And although Riley denied it, it had frightened him just as much as it had frightened Gil.

They'd set off at their regular time, crossing the empty motorway and heading towards the rest stop as they always did. As usual, Junk was trotting ahead. He knew – from long experience – that the first thing they did was look in the rubbish bin, and he was eager for any tasty morsels that might come his way.

They were nearly at the entrance to the rest stop when they stopped, their hearts bounding.

The rest stop wasn't empty. There was a car there.

It was a particularly dark night, and if the occupant of the car hadn't turned on the interior light at that moment, they might have walked right up to the vehicle without seeing it.

Riley dropped to the ground, pulling Gil with him. '*Junk!*' he hissed. 'Come back!'

There were two men in the car. Gil could see they were talking, although he immediately had the sense that their conversation was not friendly. Only one of them was looking at the other. The man in the driver's seat kept his gaze fixed ahead. He was dark haired, with a big, rubbery face, so deeply lined that his features seemed cast in perpetual shadow. He sat with his arm dangling out of the open window, his body completely still apart from the soft *tap-tap-tap* of his fingers drumming against the side of the car.

As soon as they had recovered from their shock, Riley and Gil scrambled into hiding in the bushes on the side of the verge.

'What are they doing?' Riley whispered.

'Maybe they've broken down and they're waiting for help.'

'What's *that* doing, then?' There was another car in the rest stop. Gil hadn't seen it before because it was parked right behind the first.

'They can't *both* have broken down,' Riley said. 'They must've come here in separate cars. Weird.'

'Maybe they wanted to meet up for a chat...'

'At two in the morning? On a motorway in the middle of nowhere?' Riley shook his head. 'Looks shady to me. Very shady.'

'We should go back.'

'I bet they're, like, gangsters or something,' Riley said, staring in fascination at the men in the car. 'They *look* like gang—' He broke off. 'What's Junk doing? *Junk!*'

Either Junk didn't hear him, or he was too intrigued by the *tap-tap-tap* of those fingers to pay attention. As the boys watched, helpless to prevent him, he trotted boldly forward, his tail wagging in anticipation. He reached the car and paused, gazing up at the open window.

'*Ohmygodohmygod,*' Riley muttered.

If the man in the driver's seat was surprised by Junk's sudden appearance, he didn't show it. Only his head moved, turning slightly as he shifted his gaze to the dog. It was a minor detail, but for some reason, it filled Gil with unease. Junk must have found it strange too, for he suddenly backed away from the car and padded hastily into the darkness.

'*Now* can we go?' Gil begged.

'They're leaving,' Riley said. 'Get down!'

Riley was right. The men *had* come in separate cars. Gil heard doors slamming, then both sets of headlights came on. He ducked his head, and when he looked up, the cars were gone.

'I still think we should go,' he said. 'What if they come back?'

Riley hesitated for a moment. Then he shook his head.

'We can't leave now. I'm feeling lucky tonight.'

'You always say that!'

'Well, you always say, "you always say that".'

'You can't feel lucky every night!' Gil protested.

'I didn't say I did. I said I'm feeling lucky *tonight*. You need to wash your ears out.'

Gil wanted to strangle him. But ten minutes later, the van with the cake had come along, and the sight of the cake was enough to make both boys forget all about the man with the tapping fingers.

Twenty-eight

The cake was smothered with vanilla frosting, with the words HAPPY BIRTHDAY KAYLEE! written across the top, and a pink candle in the shape of a number eight.

'I feel bad,' Grayson said, when he saw it. 'It doesn't seem right...'

'I wouldn't have taken it if I'd known it was a *birthday* cake,' Riley lied. 'It's not like I can give it back.'

'I bet Kaylee would want us to eat it,' he added cunningly. 'It's my birthday too, remember?'

'That's not for another week,' Grayson said.

'Six days and ten hours,' Riley corrected. 'Not that I'm counting.'

The cake was so big, they didn't need anything else for supper. At first, they ate around the edges, avoiding the candle and the greeting out of a lingering sense of shame. Greed soon overcame them, however, and before long, nothing was left of the cake but a small, ravaged wedge and the word HAPPY.

'We'd better not eat that, or we'll be sick,' Grayson said. Gil nodded. Even Pez looked slightly ill, and she had eaten less than anyone.

Riley gave the wedge to Junk and wiped his sticky hands on his shorts.

'I've been thinking about your story,' he told Gil. 'About the family who had the accident. It doesn't add up.'

The sugar had made Riley more argumentative than ever.

'It's just a story,' Grayson said.

'But it doesn't add up!'

'Why not?' Gil asked.

'Okay. You've got the two kids, the mum, the dad, and the dog, and they're going to Disney World, and then they crash their car which means they can't go after all. And *then*, according to you, the mum sells her necklace, and the trip is back on.'

'What's your point?'

'Simple,' Riley said, a note of triumph entering his voice. 'Dogs aren't allowed in Disney World. The Magic Kingdom wouldn't be very magic if it was full of dog poop, would it?'

'I hadn't thought of that,' Grayson said.

'Admit it,' Riley said. 'You made the whole thing up.'

'It's a support dog,' Gil said.

'A what?'

'An emotional support dog. You're allowed to take dogs like that anywhere if you need to.'

'That raggedy little thing? It couldn't even support *itself*,' Riley cried. 'It spent the whole time lying down!'

'There's no point arguing,' Gil said. 'I'm just stating the facts. It's the dad who needs the support dog. He used to be in the army, you see. His job was defusing bombs before they could explode. It took nerves of steel, but it kind of messed with his head.'

'Must have done,' Grayson agreed. 'Those guys are awesome.'

Riley clutched his head. 'I don't believe this!'

'Stop interrupting,' Grayson said. 'I want to hear more about the bombs.'

Perhaps Riley wasn't the only one with a sugar rush. Words tumbled from Gil, the story forming in his mind faster than he could speak.

Twenty-nine

The bird had been acting strangely all morning, refusing to clamber out of the dip where he roosted. Pez had tried tempting him with a particularly large cricket, but he seemed not to notice the juicy morsel. When he did finally emerge, his behaviour was even stranger. He didn't busy himself with grooming, or shuffle around pecking at the ground as he normally did. Instead, he began to pace, his head low, his eyes darting anxiously from side to side.

Birds sense changes in the weather. Perhaps it's no more than that, Pez thought. Although it was hotter than ever, with no trace of a breeze, clouds were forming in the far horizon, the big, puffy kind that could either be a signal of fair weather ahead, or just the opposite.

She decided to spend the day strengthening the fence around her vegetable garden. Keeping busy was usually a good way to avoid thinking too much. But as she hammered sticks and layered branches, her thoughts were dogs nipping at her heels, refusing to be chased away. Maybe she had picked up on the bird's unease, or maybe it was all Gil's questions that were troubling her.

Questions were like insect bites; the more you scratched them, the itchier they got. Pez knew that if she broke her silence and answered even one of Gil's questions, others would follow, each more terrible than the last.

What's your name? Where do you come from? Why did you run away?

Pez lifted the rock she was using as a hammer and brought it down on a fencepost as hard as she could, striking again and again until the wood splintered. But she couldn't drive the questions from her mind.

How could they do it? How could they do it? Didn't I matter at all?

Six months before Pez came to the island, Juno Ray made a stunning announcement. She had studied her maps and taken note of the signs and there could be no doubt. The date for the Great Return had been revealed to her. It would happen in early autumn, during a rare eclipse of the full moon.

After the initial excitement, a feeling of quiet joy settled over the Starborn. Their voices grew hushed and although they talked less, they smiled much more, and were kinder to each other than they had ever been. Since they would soon be leaving the farm for ever, there was less and less need to keep up with the chores, and they spent their time donating their few possessions to charity and in peaceful meditation.

'How are we going to get to the stars?' Pez asked her parents. 'How does it actually work?'

'That's not important,' her dad told her. 'The important thing is to believe.'

'Anything is possible as long as we believe,' her mum said.

On the night of the moon's eclipse, the Starborn were ready. They gathered on the rise behind the farm, Juno Ray in the centre, the others holding hands in a circle around her, their eyes lifted to the sky.

Pez didn't know how long they stood there, completely still, their breath clouding in the chilly air. Then someone gasped. The moon had changed shape. A vast shadow was creeping across it, swallowing it inch by inch.

Pez felt the hands of her parents tighten, as if electrified. She stared at the moon, her heart pounding with wonder. The shadow had already wiped half its face away. In a few moments it would have covered it entirely, and then... Pez squeezed her eyes shut and took a long, deep breath.

Nothing.

Nothing but the cold breeze and her numb hands. Time passed. Pez opened her eyes and gazed uncertainly around the circle. Her leg itched and she rubbed it with the heel of her foot. More time passed. Then some of the younger kids began to cry very quietly and Pez heard the whispers start.

Nobody said anything out loud. They simply slipped away in ones and twos, until only Juno Ray was left, staring at the sky. Waiting.

The weeks that followed were a dark time for the Starborn. Several members left the farm for good, others muttered behind closed doors about doing the same. Nobody saw Juno Ray. She stayed in the farmhouse and never came out. Night after night, Pez heard her mum crying.

'What did we do wrong?' her mum wept. 'We must have done *something*.'

Pez felt as miserable as everyone else. She wished she understood more about how to get to the stars. If she knew the facts, she might be able to work out what the Starborn had done wrong, and how to do it right next time.

Pez hadn't looked at her old picture books for ages, but they were still there, in an old trunk in the barn. She rummaged around until she found the one she was looking for: *The Solar System*. It was written by someone called Eleanor Friedman. Pez fetched a pencil and a piece of paper.

Dear Eleanor Friedman, she wrote. *I need some information about how people travel to the stars. Not in a spaceship, but just by themselves. Is it possible only on special days? How does that work? Also, how does believing something will happen make that thing*

*happen? Is it anything to do with magnets? Sorry for all
these questions. I'm not trying to be clever; I'm trying
to figure things out.*

Yours sincerely,

Pez hesitated, then quickly wrote her name before
she could change her mind.

There was no address for Eleanor Friedman, but
on the inside cover of the book, Pez saw the address
of the publisher. She found an envelope and a stamp –
leftover from when her mum still wrote to her family
– and the following weekend, when the Starborn went
to town to sell their small crop of pumpkins, Pez
slipped away and slid the letter into the postbox on
the corner of the street.

Pez's hand throbbed from hammering the fencepost.
The skin on her palm was starting to blister, and she
felt tired suddenly, more tired than she had ever felt
before. She dropped her stone, and even the thud as it
hit the ground sounded exhausted. Instead of finishing
the fence, she decided to go and lie down in her tepee.
It was just as hot inside, but there was shade at least.
Pez closed her eyes.

It was late afternoon, almost dusk, when she woke,
but the light was all wrong for dusk. A sickly gleam
hung over the meadow, picking out the whites of the
daisies with feverish intensity. Pez raised her eyes.
The clouds that she had noticed earlier in the day had

advanced and grown into great, blackened cliffs, flat at the top. Beneath their looming bulk, Pez saw a thin ribbon of sky, but it wasn't blue, or sunset pink.

It was green.

Before she had time to think, Pez was out of the tepee and sprinting as fast as she could across the meadow.

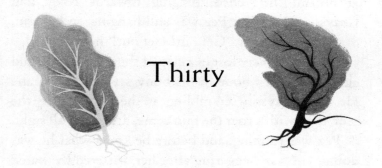

Thirty

'What's the matter?' Gil said, as Pez tugged frantically on his arm. His head had been aching all afternoon, and he was trying to keep the pain at bay by sitting as still as possible, his back against a water barrel and his eyes closed. Riley and Grayson were in their tent, although he didn't think they were asleep. The air felt too strange and charged, taut as a string pulled to the point of snapping.

Pez yanked his arm again, gesturing at the sky.

'Okay, *okay*,' he grumbled, getting to his feet. 'It's just a bit of rain.'

From nowhere, a gust of wind seized the branches of the trees, bowing them almost to the ground before a second gust sent them shuddering in the opposite direction. The sky flickered, and from the corner of his eye, Gil saw a jagged flare rip the dark, heaving belly of cloud.

He stared, confused by the silence. Then, with a flash of terror, he remembered.

Light moves faster than sound.

'Storm!' he yelled, lunging towards Riley and Grayson's tent. But Pez was still hanging on his arm, dragging him away. 'Get out! Get out!' he screamed.

His words were lost in a clap of thunder so loud and close that every bone in his body seemed to vibrate. He saw Grayson scrambling at the entrance to the tent, then with a roar the rain came, drowning all sight.

Pez was running, and before he knew what he was doing, Gil was staggering after her, battered by water, the rain so dense it was almost solid, filling his mouth so that he had to spit to breathe. He couldn't see or hear the others. Even Pez was no more than a vague shape, though she was barely an arm's length ahead. A bolt of lightning hit the ground somewhere behind him and he saw them for an instant, Grayson's arm around his brother, Riley's mouth open in a shout.

Pez was heading for the trees. *That's wrong*, Gil thought, although his legs kept running. *It's not safe under trees in a storm.* But he was already among them, the vast noise of the rain joined by the rattle and thud of wind-whipped branches and the creak of aching wood.

A shape loomed ahead, glinting darkly, rain drumming against it with a metallic patter.

The car. The one that Riley and Grayson had filled with provisions and hidden so that nobody could see it from the road. Gil had forgotten about it, but Pez hadn't. He reached for the door handle, almost choking with relief. Pez was already in the back seat, moving tins and bags of food on to the floor to make room for herself. Riley and Grayson came hurtling through the trees, and then they were all in the car with the doors slammed shut.

For a moment, everyone was too busy gasping for breath to speak.

'Holy *cow*,' Grayson said.

Lightning flashed beyond the trees, where they had been. Gil caught a glimpse of writhing branches, water pouring in an unbroken torrent down the windscreen of the car.

'Are we safe here?' Grayson asked.

'I think so, unless…' Gil's voice trailed off. He'd been about to say, 'unless a tree falls on us,' but decided against it. Everyone was already far too frightened.

'Lucky we found the car,' Grayson said.

'It wasn't luck,' Gil said. 'It was Pez. She saved us. She—'

He was interrupted by a strangled cry from the back seat.

'Junk!' Riley yelled. 'We left Junk behind!'

Lightning forked again, directly ahead, and as if in answer, the rain redoubled in strength, pounding on the roof of the car with a roar to match the thunder.

'We left Junk!'

'He'll be okay,' Gil said. 'I'm sure he'll be okay.'

'He won't!' Riley's voice rose to a howl. 'I have to get him. I have to find him!'

'You *can't*…'

Riley was struggling with the door, trying to push it open against the wind.

'Stop him!' Gil cried to Grayson. But Riley was already outside. Gil saw him bent double as he staggered away.

If Grayson hesitated, it was only for a split-second. 'I'll get him back,' he said, his voice oddly calm. 'You stay here, you promise?' And before Gil could answer or protest, he was gone.

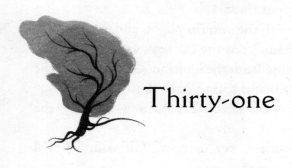

Thirty-one

Gil peered frantically through the window, both hands pressed to the cold glass.

'Can you see them?' he cried. 'What if they don't come back? What if they *die* out there?' His voice rose in panic. He tried to stop, to breathe, but the panic was too quick and strong. His body juddered with the force of it. 'What are we g-going to d-do?' he stuttered.

He felt Pez touch his shoulder and he stilled, partly from surprise and partly because the touch itself was so gentle, so utterly steady. She was trying to reassure him, Gil knew, and at the same time – he didn't know how he knew this, but he did – at the same time trying to reassure herself too. To say, without speaking, that they were both in this together.

He fetched a deep breath. 'I'm okay,' he said, and found that he meant it.

'Grayson told us to stay here,' he said. 'But maybe

we can help. We need to find the car keys. Where do you think they put them?'

Gil groped for the interior light and switched it on. The boys hadn't put the car keys anywhere. They were still dangling from the ignition. Gil turned on the engine, praying that it hadn't gone flat.

It fired at once, headlights cutting through the driving rain.

'They'll be able to see us now,' Gil said. 'They'll know which direction to run.'

Something banged on the top of the car, and he flinched. 'It was only a branch,' he said. 'I bet it didn't even leave a dent.'

A lurching shape appeared in the headlights and vanished.

'Was that —' Before Gil could say his name, Grayson had hurled himself into the back seat, and Riley was scrabbling at the passenger door. Gil leaned over and yanked him inside.

'The li-li-lightning,' Riley babbled, his teeth chattering. 'It came so close I heard it *sizzle*.'

'You found him!' Riley was clutching Junk with both arms. The dog was trembling so violently that his entire body vibrated.

'He won't stop shaking,' Riley said. 'I need a blanket to wrap him in.'

'Everything's gone,' Grayson said. 'The washing line, the tents…'

They were all shaking now, as if they had only just realised how wet and cold they were.

'It'll get warm soon,' Gil said. 'The windows are already fogging up.'

'At least we've got food,' Riley said. 'I'm starving. What can you find back there, Gray?'

Grayson rummaged on the floor of the car. 'Two tins of frankfurters, no, hang on...' He peered at the label, tracing the words with his finger. '*Mini* frankfurters,' he corrected. 'That's fancy.'

'Doesn't matter how fancy they are, we don't have a tin opener, remember?'

Gil switched off the engine and reached in his pocket for his penknife.

'Yes, we do.'

They passed the tins from hand to hand, taking turns to fish for the pale, flabby, yet mysteriously delicious sausages, Junk gulping his share eagerly, his fear forgotten. They were warmer now, their clothes drying fast, although from the sound of it, the storm had lost none of its fury.

'I guess we're here for the night,' Grayson said.

Riley poked Gil's arm. 'Tell us a story. Did that stupid family ever get to Disney World?'

'They're there now,' Gil said. 'There's a storm there too. It caught them by surprise. They'd just got on a roller coaster when it hit. They were the only people on the ride, and as they were going through a tunnel, the power cut. So right now, they're sitting in the dark, wondering what to do next. Problem is, nobody knows they're there...'

Gil kept talking, although he could tell from the

silence in the back seat that Grayson and Pez had fallen asleep. A few moments later, Riley's head lolled and even Junk finally closed his eyes.

Gil leaned back, listening to the wind and rain. Despite his damp clothes and cramped legs, a sense of great comfort came over him. He reached for the hagstone around his neck, feeling its reassuring weight against his palm. They were no more than a pinprick of light amid the storm. But they were safe. They were together.

Thirty-two

Gil woke to the sound of Junk scratching to get out of the car. The sun had risen, and the sky was such a clear and innocent blue that for half a second, he wondered whether the storm had been nothing but a terrifying dream.

Pez must have crept away without waking them. Only Grayson was left in the back seat, fast asleep, his hand still curled around an empty tin of mini frankfurters.

Gil nudged Riley. 'Hey.'

'Wasn't me,' Riley mumbled.

'Wake up.' Gil nudged him again. 'Junk needs to get out.'

'Where am I?' Grayson said, his voice bleary.

Riley opened the door and Junk shot away. The others followed more slowly, stretching their stiff legs. Apart from the mud and the leaves scattered everywhere, the storm didn't seem to have done much damage. It was only when the boys emerged from the trees that they saw the full extent of the wreckage.

The meadow was a sea of mangled grass and torn petals. Branches littered the ground, filling the air with the fresh sap smell of wounded trees. Grayson had been right about the tents. They were gone, blown clean away, still trailing their ropes and pegs. And with them had gone the tarp, the sleeping bags and whatever clothes had been lying around when the storm descended. The rest of the boys' possessions lay scattered far and wide, drenched and smeared with mud.

'My backpack,' Gil said.

It took him several minutes to find it, wedged in a bush. He tugged it free and carried it dripping, back to the others. Grayson had located their tin-can stools and set them up around the remains of the fireplace. The three boys sat for a while in shocked, forlorn silence, like shipwreck survivors on an alien shore.

'We're done for,' Riley said at last.

Gil reached into his sodden backpack, searching for the picture of his parents. It was stuck to the bottom, and when he pulled it out, the paper split and part of the surface of the photograph peeled away. Gil laid what was left of it on a nearby rock.

'It'll be all right once it dries,' Grayson told him, although Gil knew he was only being kind.

'We're done for,' Riley repeated. 'We'll have to go home.'

I thought this *was our home,* Gil wanted to say, but he knew how childish it would sound. Even without the storm, they would have had to leave the island sooner or later. When their food ran out or when the summer ended, and the weather grew too cold. The island had never been their home. They had only been pretending it was, like little kids under the kitchen table, making a house out of blankets and pillows.

'We should go and see if Pez is okay,' Gil said, his heart heavy.

Her camp was not nearly as badly damaged as theirs. Although the fence around the vegetable plot lay flat, and the tub of crickets had been knocked on its side, the rest of her possessions were safe inside the hollow tree and her tepee was battered but standing. She had made the right choice to build her camp there, protected by trees. *Pez is always a step ahead*, Gil thought. He peered into the tepee. Apart from the bottle in the shape of the Eiffel Tower, half-covered now with leaves, it was empty.

'Where is she?' Riley said. 'Where's she gone?'

Pez hadn't gone anywhere. She was simply sitting so still that it was a while before they noticed her, with her back to a tree and her knees pulled up to her chin.

'There you are!' Gil said. 'I thought for a minute you—'

He broke off. There were tears running down Pez's face.

'What's the matter?' Her headband – the one she had made for her precious gold earring – was resting at a crooked angle. For some reason, the sight of it upset Gil even more than her tears.

Like a princess whose crown has slipped, he thought. *Too sad to set it right again.*

'What's the matter?' he repeated, falling to his knees beside her. 'It's not so bad. I know your fence has fallen down, but you can repair it, can't you?'

Gil gazed anxiously at her tear-streaked face.

'You can catch more crickets. I'll help. We'll *all* help, right?' Gil glanced at the others, standing awkwardly nearby.

''Course, yeah,' Grayson muttered.

'Totally,' Riley added.

But Gil could see it was no use. The lost crickets weren't the problem. And it wasn't the holes in her tepee, or even the flattened vegetable patch. He knew that none of these things were enough to make Pez cry.

'Where's the bird?' Grayson said. 'The condor?'

Gil stared around the empty camp. 'It's not here. It must have flown off.'

At his words, Pez buried her face in her knees and broke into sobs.

Thirty-three

He had gone. He had left her. Pez didn't know how many times she had told the bird to fly away, but she had never meant it. She knew that now. That was why she had gone on feeding him. Stroking his feathers, sitting beside him, thinking about him night and day. It hadn't been enough. She hadn't been enough. Pez felt her heart break into a thousand pieces and drift away, as weightless as dandelion seeds borne on the breeze.

The bird had rejected her, just like everyone else.

Pez had had no idea if her letter would ever get to its destination, or if it did, whether anyone would bother reading it. She still wondered about it from time to time as the weeks passed, but it was certainly not on her mind when, a month later, Juno Ray called for a meeting of all the remaining Starborn.

They gathered in the barn. Apart from her two assistants, nobody had seen Juno Ray since the night of the eclipse, and there was an air of great anxiety as they waited for her arrival. When she finally appeared, Pez was surprised – and relieved – to see how well she looked, almost peaceful, her small hands hidden in the folds of a silvery gown that glimmered in the dim light.

'I have something to share with you,' Juno Ray said as she seated herself. She took an envelope from her lap and held it up for everyone to see. 'This,' she said, 'arrived yesterday.' She paused dramatically, her gaze sweeping the barn.

Pez had no clue what she was talking about. It wasn't until Juno Ray reached into the envelope and pulled out a piece of paper, that she guessed the truth. The blood rushed to her head. Eleanor Friedman, author of *The Solar System*, had written back to her. Until that moment, it hadn't occurred to Pez that the letter would be delivered to the farmhouse. *I ought to have known*, she thought wretchedly. *Where else could it have gone but straight to Juno Ray?*

'This letter was addressed to one among us,' Juno Ray said. 'After deep consideration I made the decision to open it.'

She paused again, as if gathering her strength.

'I will share only part of it,' she said at last. 'And I must warn you to prepare yourselves...'

Silence fell over the barn. Juno Ray cleared her throat.

'*Your letter was full of interesting questions,*' she read. '*The easiest to answer is the one concerning space travel. The fact is that the stars cannot be reached, even in a spaceship because they are too far away. We would need to travel faster than the speed of light which is impossible because light is the fastest thing in the whole universe...*'

Gasps and anguished mutterings filled the barn. Juno Ray held up her hand for quiet.

'*Even though light moves incredibly quickly,*' she continued, '*most stars are so far away that it takes hundreds and hundreds of years for their light to reach the earth. Which means we have no way of knowing if a star is still there. Although we can see its light, it may have vanished centuries ago. It's possible – although very unlikely – that there are no stars left in the sky at all!*'

Cries of distress rose all around. Pez's mum made a whimpering noise and clapped her hand to her mouth. Pez hardly noticed. Her brain was on fire with what she had just learned. If Eleanor Friedman was right – and Pez didn't see any reason why she shouldn't be – the mystery of the Great Return was solved. The Starborn had failed to travel to the stars, not because there was an error in their preparations, but because *it simply couldn't be done*!

'So, now we know.' Juno Ray's gaze fell on Pez for the first time.

'Step forward.'

Pez did as she was told, her heart sinking. Now

everyone would realise it was she who had sent the letter. They would say she was a show-off, trying – as usual – to be clever. Perhaps she shouldn't have expected any different. It must be difficult for Juno Ray – difficult and embarrassing – to admit she had made such a huge mistake – telling everyone they could travel to the stars, when in fact they couldn't.

But Juno Ray didn't look embarrassed. There was an odd expression on her face. *It's not happiness*, Pez thought, staring at her in confusion. *It's more like... triumph.*

'So, now we know,' Juno Ray repeated. She pressed her hands on the arms of her chair and slowly rose to her feet, the folds of her gown falling like a curtain around her.

'On the night of the Great Return, our circle was broken,' Juno Ray said. 'Is it any wonder that we failed?'

Pez gaped at her, too astonished to speak, or even shake her head in protest.

'We had a doubter among us!' Juno Ray's voice rose to a cry. 'One who believed so little in the truth that she went for answers to an ignorant outsider, *a scientist*!'

Juno Ray paused to let her words sink in. Heads began to nod, followed by a growing murmur of agreement.

'*I didn't...*' Pez whispered. '*It wasn't...*'

Feet shuffled. People were moving away from her, as though afraid.

'We will try again,' Juno Ray was saying. 'And we

will succeed. But only if we separate ourselves from the ugliness of doubt. Doubt is a disease. We must protect ourselves against it, whatever the cost.'

Pez turned to her parents, her eyes filling with tears of bewilderment and fear. 'Tell them it isn't true,' she said. 'I didn't do anything; it was only a letter…' Her mum's mouth trembled for an instant, then she pressed her lips together.

'I won't do it again,' Pez wept. 'I *promise.*'

But her parents weren't looking at her. They were staring straight ahead as though transformed – as people are transformed in nightmares – into terrifying strangers. Then, as everyone else had done, they stepped away and Pez was alone.

A pit opened in her stomach, so deep it felt she might fall for ever. Her parents should have spoken up and defended her. Instead, by keeping silent, they had shown whose side they were on. Later, perhaps, they might relent. Given time to think things through properly, they might change their minds. But Pez didn't give them that time. It was too late. It wasn't just that her parents had betrayed her. By choosing Juno Ray's lies over the truth, they had betrayed the world itself. The world of rules and reason. The world Pez loved.

That evening, while the Starborn were busy ignoring her, Pez stole everything she needed. A collection of essential tools, seeds for planting, cooking equipment and enough money for a bus – any bus – that would take her as far from the farm as possible.

She didn't need her parents, or Juno Ray, or the rest of the Starborn. She didn't need anyone. Only the bird, and now even he was gone.

Thirty-four

Gil stared helplessly at Pez, not knowing what to say.

'Kind of stupid of that bird, if you ask me,' Riley said. 'Flying off in the middle of a storm.'

'We didn't ask you!' Gil said, giving him a furious look.

'I'm only saying.'

'Well, don't!'

'But it *is* stupid,' Riley persisted. 'Birds are supposed to be smart, aren't they, Gray?'

'Supposed to be,' Grayson agreed.

'Bet you anything it didn't fly away,' Riley said. 'Bet you it's hiding somewhere.'

Pez tightened her grip on her knees, her knuckles white.

Riley raised his hand to the side of his mouth. 'Bird!' he hollered. 'Hey, bird! Come out, come out, wherever you are!'

'Shut up!' Gil yelled, leaping to his feet with clenched fists. 'Stop messing around. Can't you see—'

He was interrupted by a commotion in the bushes. There was a loud rustling noise and the sound of snapping twigs. Then the leaves parted.

'Told you!' Riley crowed.

The condor was in a pitiful state of disarray, his chest stuck with burrs and his wing feathers sticking out in all directions. He took a sheepish step forward, ducked his head, and began furiously preening himself.

If Gil expected Pez to jump up and rush to greet the bird, he was disappointed. All she did was give it a quick look. But for a second, he saw her eyes light with joy. Then she wiped her face with the back of her hand and marched off to inspect the vegetable plot.

Although it seemed ridiculous that such an odd, ungainly creature could be the bringer of good luck, things immediately started to get better after the condor reappeared.

When Pez – helped by Grayson – lifted the fence that had fallen on the vegetable plot, there was far less damage than they'd expected. The fence had flattened the young plants, breaking many of their stems, but it had also protected them from the worst of the wind and rain, and with care they would recover.

Then Riley, making a tour of the island's perimeter, saw a red shape caught in the branches of a tree. It was one of the sleeping bags. As he was climbing up to get it, he spotted a second sleeping bag, half-submerged in the pond. It was covered with slime and mud, but after the storm there was no shortage of water, and they rinsed both sleeping bags and laid them to dry in the sun.

Encouraged by these finds, the three boys criss-crossed the island, searching for more of their missing possessions. Most of their clothes were gone for good, along with their washing line, the pink vanity bag full of hair curlers and the third sleeping bag. But they managed to retrieve almost everything else, including Grayson's wooden teaspoons, still safe in their roll of fabric.

'The good news is I found the camping stove,' Riley announced. 'Bad news is that it's trashed. We must've stepped on it when we were running around last night.'

'Probably Gray,' he added. 'It's totally bent out of shape.'

'Sorry,' Grayson muttered, glancing with shame at his feet.

'Doesn't matter, we can't light it anyway,' Riley said. 'Can't find either of our lighters.'

'Don't we have matches?' Gil asked.

'Sure, we do.' Riley rolled his eyes. 'Underneath a load of mud.'

Gloom descended on them again.

'It's no good if we can't start a fire,' Grayson said. 'I guess that settles it.'

'Pez has a flint,' Gil protested. 'She'd lend it to us. And we could try using the magnifying glass on my penknife...'

'It's not only that,' Riley pointed out. 'We lost the tents, remember? We can't stay here if we don't have anywhere to sleep.'

'So, you're just going to leave?'

There was a long silence. Neither Riley nor Grayson could meet Gil's eye. He stared around the meadow. The grass was still battered, but it was less flat than before, already starting to spring back.

'We don't need tents,' he said suddenly. 'The storm took them away, but it left us something even better.'

'A campervan?' Riley said, in his most sarcastic voice. 'One of those fancy ones with little curtains and fake leather seats?'

'Branches,' Gil said. 'It left us branches. Loads of them.'

The boys would never have been able to make a single tepee, let alone three, if Pez hadn't been there to teach them. She showed them how to mark out a circle and form a tripod using three long branches, their ends set deep in the ground, their forked tops wedged tight. Then, little by little, they began filling in the walls with smaller branches, laced with brush and twigs. There were gaps which they would have to close using stones and moss and whatever else they could find, but by the end of the day, the tepees were finished enough to sleep in.

Since there were only two sleeping bags, the boys agreed to share, drawing lots to decide who would get to use them. But the night was warm and the bags weren't really needed. *They just add to the cosiness*, Gil thought, as he snuggled down in his new bed. He looked up. Stars filled the cracks in his tepee, and in the largest gap, a bright silver wedge of the moon.

With the tents, they had only been camping, he decided. And their life on the island had felt like a temporary thing. But the tepees were solid and unmoving, built to last longer than a day, or a week, or even a month. They turned the island from a place to visit into a place to *live*.

Gil closed his eyes. *We could stay here. We could be here for as long as we want.* Then he remembered. Wasn't it just when he thought he could stay in a place that Ms Lundy had invariably arrived to take him away? He should know that by now. Thinking he'd found a home was always the beginning of the end.

Later, he would understand he was wrong. Building the tepees wasn't the beginning of the end, because that had already happened. Perhaps it was the night they stole the cake, or the fact that the storm left them with two sleeping bags instead of three. Or maybe the beginning of the end had been there all along, for a simple reason:

Because Riley always had to be the worst person around.

Thirty-five

The next few days were the happiest Gil had felt since arriving on the island. The weather was glorious, with a light breeze and cloudless skies. The boys spent most of the time improving their tepees until they were as wind and water resistant as possible.

Riley was particularly proud of his tepee. He had decorated it with sharpened sticks that jutted out in all directions like an angry hedgehog.

'Makes a change not having to listen to Gray snoring all night,' he said as they sat around the fire.

'I don't snore,' Grayson said.

'Okay, but your feet smell.' Riley pulled a scrap of blackened wood from the fire and blew on it to cool it down. He had cut a square from an old shirt and was making a pirate flag for the top of his tepee, using soot to draw the skull and crossbones.

'I hope you can take that down in a hurry if we have to do the drill,' Grayson said.

Riley shrugged. ''Course I can.'

Now that the tents were gone, the boys had a new drill for covering their tracks in the event of an intruder, but they had only practised it a couple of times. There was something about the tepees that gave them a feeling of security, as if they could afford to be careless because they didn't need to worry any longer.

While Riley was busy adorning his tepee and constructing another – smaller but just as snug – for Junk to sleep in, Gil, Grayson and Pez worked on a gift for Riley's birthday. The gift had been Gil's idea, although Grayson and Pez did most of the work, toiling for hours in secret to get it ready in time.

After loudly counting down the hours and days until his birthday, Riley was strangely bashful when it finally arrived. He sat drinking his morning coffee, saying nothing, staring at Gil and Grayson and then back again at Gil, with a look of anticipation on his face, waiting for them to wish him a happy birthday.

'Well, I don't *feel* any different,' he said at last.

'Why would you?' Grayson said.

'Yeah, why would you?' Gil echoed, trying not to grin.

There was a silence. Riley took an anxious sip of coffee. 'So, what are we doing today?' he said, his voice lifting in a futile attempt to sound casual. 'Anyone got plans?'

'Not that I know of,' Grayson said. 'You got any plans, Gil?'

Gil shook his head. 'Same old, same old.'

'Why'd you ask?' Grayson said.

'You *know* why!' Riley yelled, finally losing all self-control. 'You're pretending, right? You haven't *really* forgotten it's my birthday! Stop laughing!'

''Course we didn't forget,' Grayson said, still chuckling.

'How could we?' Gil added.

'Where's my present, then?' Riley demanded.

'You'll have to wait until lunchtime for that,' Grayson said.

Pez had Riley's present at her camp. It was a picnic hamper. She had woven it like her fence, except with smaller sticks. It was crude-looking and slightly crooked, but it had four sides and a lid that opened, just like a real picnic hamper.

Inside were four napkins, washed and folded, that Gil had cut out of a T-shirt and four mugs made from tins. He had scratched names on the tins with the point of his knife, so that everyone knew which was theirs. There was no pepper available, but the bottle in the shape of the Eiffel Tower held salt. It was too big to be a proper saltshaker, but it was still dainty.

There were four peaches in the hamper, along with four sandwiches made with slices of fried potato instead of bread and the last of the mini frankfurters, flavoured with hot sauce from a sachet found in the rest stop rubbish bin. And there were Grayson's teaspoons which he had finished the night before. The cricket, the frog, the crow, and the condor – one for each of them.

Riley stared at the picnic for a long time, not touching anything.

'It's so fancy,' he kept saying. 'It's so… *fancy.*' And then, 'You *made* all this?'

Grayson spread the sleeping bags and they settled down to eat, Riley still overwhelmed by awe. He sat with his back very straight and his hands folded neatly in his lap, his face as solemn as if he were seated at the grandest of all grand banquets. Gil passed him the bottle in the shape of the Eiffel Tower, and Riley took it reverently, with the tips of his fingers, as if it might shatter at the smallest touch. He tapped a few grains of salt on to the edge of his sandwich and took a tiny nibble.

'What's the matter?' Grayson said. 'Don't you like it?'

'I want to make it last,' Riley said.

Grayson, who had been about to take an enormous bite, closed his mouth, and without saying anything, everyone began to eat as slowly as Riley, as if each mouthful of sandwich was a whole course, to be deeply and thoughtfully savoured.

At last, they were finished, and Pez filled their tin mugs with tea. She must have brewed it from flowers of some sort, because it tasted like perfume, neither sweet nor earthy but somewhere perfectly in between.

They stirred the tea with Grayson's spoons – although it didn't need stirring – and sipped and stirred again.

'This is the best picnic of my whole life,' Riley said.

Gil could have pointed out that it was the *only* picnic of his whole life, but he had the feeling that Riley didn't mean that. He wasn't saying this was the best picnic that he'd ever had, but the best that he would *ever* have, even if he lived to be a hundred.

Gil smiled. 'Happy birthday.'

'Yeah, happy birthday,' Grayson said. They raised their mugs and chinked them together, even Pez joining in the toast.

'I said I didn't feel any different today, but I lied,' Riley announced at last, with a return to his normal swagger. 'I feel even more lucky than usual.'

'What do you mean?' Gil asked.

'I mean I'm going to the rest stop tonight and I'm going to find another sleeping bag. Or a couple of blankets at least. Loads of cars have blankets in the back.'

Grayson made a face. 'You don't have to do that. It's your birthday.'

'That's *why* I have to do it! I'm sick of sharing those stupid sleeping bags. Gray always cheats when we draw lots because he can read my mind. He fixes it so I never get a bag.'

'That's ridiculous,' Gil said, although part of him wondered if Riley was right. Not about the cheating but about Grayson being able to read his brother's mind. He remembered the night he had arrived on the island, and how the boys kept saying the same thing when they played Rock, Paper, Scissors.

'Nobody can read minds, it's impossible,' Gil said, trying to convince himself.

Riley shrugged. 'Whatever, I'm still going.'

'I don't think you should,' Gil said, although he wasn't sure why he suddenly felt so strongly. Perhaps it was because the day had been going so well and asking for more seemed dangerous – too much like tempting fate.

'What about we have an extra-long story tonight instead?' he ventured.

'About that family, I suppose,' Riley scoffed. 'Let me guess, a baby fell from the top of Cinderella's castle, and they saved it and as a reward, Mickey Mouse gave them a thousand dollars to spend in the gift shop, and instead of getting stuff for themselves like normal people...' Riley's voice rose to a mocking shout, 'THEY BOUGHT EVERYONE IN DISNEY WORLD A STUPID LOLLIPOP!'

'Can Mickey Mouse do that?' Grayson asked. 'I mean, is that even a thing?'

But Riley was not to be distracted. He turned to Gil. 'Are you going to come with me tonight or not?'

Gil shook his head.

'Then I guess it's just me and Junk,' Riley said.

Thirty-six

That night, Gil dreamed he was standing on a wide beach, watching his parents as they paddled away in their kayaks. He waved his arms above his head, but his parents weren't looking at him, and when he tried to yell, no sound came out.

I've got a good feeling about this!

Ms Lundy was standing beside him. She was waving at his parents too, but she wasn't trying to get their attention. She was waving goodbye.

Don't worry, Gil, she said. *I'm sure it will be fine this time!*

He woke with a small cry, and lay staring at the dark, the dream still wrapped around him. The anniversary of his parents' death was coming up. Perhaps that was why he had dreamed about them.

Even though Gil had only been five years old at the time, he knew the date because there was a calendar stuck to the fridge and his mum had drawn a smiley face in the space for that day, below the number twenty-three. It was the last mark she'd made on the calendar. That was why Gil had remembered it. Because there was nothing but blank spaces after that smiley face. Nothing but a series of empty days.

He burrowed deeper into his bag, although he didn't close his eyes because he had the feeling that the dream wasn't done with him. Something terrible was waiting if he went back to sleep too soon.

Dawn was still hours away, and the dark was deep and filled with secret sound, the murmur of leaves and the rustle of tiny bodies. Gil settled himself, and his breath grew steady as he listened, the dream slowly fading until it was no more than a vague shadow in the back of his mind. He was about to fall asleep again when he felt a soft vibration in the earth beneath his cheek, and his eyes snapped wide.

Riley was coming back. He was running, feet thudding against the ground. Nearer he came, and now Gil could hear him panting, a frantic gasping sound, drawing closer to a sob with every breath. A torch turned on, moving erratically as if held in a shaking hand.

'What's the matter? What happened?' It was Grayson's voice. Gil scrambled out of his tepee on hands and knees, blinded for a second in the beam of Grayson's torch. Then the light swung away and found Riley's face.

'What's wrong?' Gil cried.

Riley was breathing too hard to speak. He was carrying something – a bag – the handle gripped in his fist.

TANIA UNSWORTH

'What happened?' Grayson repeated.

'Something... really... bad,' Riley gasped, looking desperately left and right. 'Where's Junk? Where is he?'

'He's here,' Grayson said, resting his hand on the dog's head.

'What do you mean, something bad?' Gil said. Riley had begun to shake as if freezing cold. Grayson made him sit down. Then he fetched the sleeping bag from his tepee and wrapped it around his brother's shoulders.

'Do you want me to make a fire?'

'It's not safe.' Riley's voice rose in panic. 'Someone might see...'

'Who?'

'The man.' Riley looked at Gil. 'The man from the other night... the one with dark hair, sitting in the driver's seat. Remember?'

Gil nodded. 'He was there again,' Riley said. 'Both men were.'

'Already in the rest stop?'

Riley nodded. 'The two cars were parked like before, only the men were outside, just kind of standing around and talking. I ducked behind the bin and Junk did too. He lay completely flat. I didn't have to tell him to do that, he knew he had to stay hidden. I've always said he's the smartest dog in the world, and now I have proof.'

'Okay,' Gil said. 'He's the smartest dog in the world, but you still haven't told us what happened.'

Riley drew the sleeping bag tighter, his body rocking with anxiety. 'I told you the men were talking only I couldn't hear what they were saying, and then the man with dark hair grabbed the other guy's neck, although it wasn't his neck, it was more like the collar of his shirt, it just looked like his neck because he was holding so tight...'

'Take a breath,' Grayson said, interrupting Riley's babble. 'That's it, nice and slow.'

'He was right in the other guy's face,' Riley continued, after a pause. 'I thought he'd start yelling, but he didn't. It was the opposite of that. His voice went low and kind of calm, scary calm.'

'Make one more mistake,' the dark-haired man said, 'and I'll kill you.'

Riley reached for Junk's snout and held it shut, desperately willing the dog to remain still. When he and Gil had seen the men before, he'd suspected they were up to no good. But suspecting something was completely different from knowing for sure. Riley's heart began to pound, faster and faster, until there were no spaces at all between the beats, only a single, bursting pressure.

'I'll kill you,' the dark-haired man repeated. 'Got it?'

'I got it, I got it,' his companion cried, his voice ragged with fear. 'I won't do it again...'

He staggered back, clutching his throat, and Riley watched him hurry to his car and peel out of the rest stop with a squeal of brakes.

'What about the other man?' Gil asked. 'Did he leave too?'

'Not right away,' Riley said. 'He lit a cigarette and walked over to the trees and smoked it. Then he came back and got into his car and drove off.'

'He didn't see you,' Grayson said. 'You're a hundred per cent sure?'

'If he'd seen me, do you think I'd be sitting here?'

'So, it's okay,' Gil said. 'No harm done.'

Riley gave them an anguished look and clasped his head between his hands. 'It's not okay. It doesn't matter that he didn't see me. He's going to come looking for me anyway.'

'Why?' Grayson said. And then, 'Oh, Riley...'

'What did you do?' Gil said, although he suddenly wasn't sure he wanted to know.

Riley's head was bent so low that he was talking to his knees. 'It was when he was smoking,' he mumbled. 'He had his back to me. I don't know why I did it. Habit, I guess...'

'You took something from his car, didn't you?' Gil said. 'You took that bag!'

It was lying on the ground nearby, where Riley had dropped it. A large gym bag, made from dark-coloured nylon, with a zipper at the top. Riley nudged it miserably with the tip of his foot. 'I didn't know what was inside, I wouldn't have taken it if I'd known!'

Grayson reached for the bag, unzipped it, and slowly swung the beam of his torch over the contents.

'Yeah,' he said, in a stunned voice. 'He's coming back for sure.'

Thirty-seven

There were two hundred and fifty thousand dollars in the gym bag. They were in bundles of five thousand; fifty bundles in all. Grayson counted them out carefully and replaced them in the bag. Dawn had come, and Riley, in a pitiful effort to atone for his crime, had gathered wood, lit the fire, and was now boiling water for coffee.

Gil went to fetch Pez. She was in her tepee, her blanket wrapped tight, her hand clutching the edge of it as she slept, as if to pull it still closer.

'Something's happened,' Gil whispered.

She sat up at once, her eyes wide.

'We have to have a meeting,' Gil said. 'We have to figure out what to do.'

She gazed at him steadily as he explained, her face serene, even when he told her how much money there was in the bag. *She shot down the drone, and found us shelter from the storm*, Gil thought. If anyone could help them now, surely it was her. Then he remembered the shadowed face of the driver, and the *tap-tap-tap* of his fingers against the side of the car. If it came to a showdown, Gil knew they'd be in real trouble. Even with Pez on their side.

They joined the others by the fire. 'This is what I think,' Grayson said, as soon as they all had their coffee. 'I think Riley's right – that man is going to want his bag back. He must have been trying to figure out where he lost it from the moment he saw it wasn't in the back of his car any more. But we don't know when that was. Maybe it was straight away, or maybe he stopped at a couple of other places before he noticed.'

'Maybe he *still* hasn't noticed,' Gil said.

'Maybe. We can't count on that. We've got to assume he saw straight away, and he knows the bag was taken at the rest stop.'

Gil had never heard Grayson speak with such confidence and authority. He even looked older, as if he had grown up overnight – further from being a boy, and closer to being a man.

'So, what do we do?' Gil said.

'I think we should wait until night and leave the bag at the rest stop where the man can find it, and then get in our car and drive away.'

'You mean, give it back?' Riley said, breaking his silence at last. 'Why can't we take it with us?'

'It doesn't belong to us.'

'Well, it doesn't belong to him either. I'm sure it's stolen. You can't steal something that's already stolen…'

'It doesn't belong to us,' Grayson said again.

Gil expected Riley to keep arguing, but his spirit seemed to have evaporated.

'Why do we have to go?' Gil said. 'Why can't we just leave the bag at the rest stop? He won't come after us once he's got it back.'

'I wouldn't bet on it,' Riley said, shaking his head. 'If he finds the bag, he'll know someone was watching him. He won't like that. What if he decides to hang around and find out who it was?'

'That's why our best bet is to dump the money and leave,' Grayson said. 'He'll know he was seen, but by that time we'll be miles away. There's no chance he'll find us.'

'I guess you're right,' Gil said, his shoulders slumping.

'It's a pity,' Grayson said. 'We could've stayed here for a bit longer.'

Maybe for ever, Gil thought. It wasn't fair. The island was their place. And now, after everything they'd been through, just when it was beginning to feel like home, they would have to leave it all behind. He caught Pez's eye.

'If we go, will you come with us?'

She hesitated, then shook her head. Gil knew she would rather stay and take her chances. She was good at hiding. If the man came looking, the boys' abandoned camp would likely be all he'd find...

'There's another option,' Riley said. 'What if we don't give the money back and we don't leave?'

Grayson shook his head. '*Riley*...'

'Hear me out, okay? Let's say he knows the bag was taken at the rest stop. That means he's going to come back and have a look around. And he's going to figure out that whoever took the bag didn't leave straight away in a car, because he didn't see another car. That doesn't mean whoever took it wasn't picked up later, or hitched a ride, or just ran off. For all he knows, someone could have been following him – someone who already knew he had that money.'

'I guess,' Grayson admitted unwillingly. 'But—'

'Think about it!' Riley jumped up and began pacing rapidly to and fro, as if trying to catch up with his own speeding thoughts. 'Why would he – why would *anyone* – think that whoever took that money was still hanging around? He doesn't know we're living here. Who lives in the middle of a motorway? It's not even going to cross his mind.'

'That's a good point,' Gil said.

'He'll come back, have a look around, and then go away,' Riley said. 'He may have already come back. Which is why returning the money is a dumb idea – because if he comes back a second time, he'll know for sure we're still in the area. If he doesn't, someone else will find the money, and we'll have left the island for nothing.'

'I don't like it,' Grayson said. 'This is bad stuff. This is about as bad as it gets.'

'Which is why my plan makes sense,' Riley argued. 'We'll be safe if we lie low for a few days. Stay on the island and not even *think* of going near the rest stop.'

'I don't like it,' Grayson said again.

'But I told you, we'll be safe!'

'We'll be safer if we leave.'

'Let's vote on it,' Riley said. 'Who thinks we should stay?' He raised his hand.

'Pez?' She nodded. 'That's two votes to stay,' Riley said.

Everyone looked at Gil. He frowned, trying to think through the logic of Riley's argument. There were too many what-ifs, too many things they couldn't be sure of. Grayson's plan was the safest. It was also the right thing to do. Grayson always did the right thing. They should get rid of the money. It didn't belong to them.

But this was their home, and he had nowhere else to go, and worst of all, they would have to leave Pez behind. Gil didn't think he could do that.

'I'm sorry, Grayson,' he said. 'I vote we stay too.'

There was a long silence. Then Grayson nodded. 'Okay,' he said. 'We stay and we keep the money. For *now*. Like Riley says, that guy probably won't come looking for us. But if he does, we need to be ready.'

Thirty-eight

Grayson was right. They needed to be ready, although it took a while to decide on the best strategy. At first, Riley wanted to turn the island into a fortress. They could set traps, he suggested, hidden pits with sharpened sticks at the bottom. Or use the bag of money as bait, hanging it from a tree in a cunning way so that the minute it was touched, a noose would tighten around the intruder's ankle, jerk him off his feet, and leave him dangling upside down.

'How would we dig the pits?' Grayson pointed out. 'All we've got is Pez's gardening trowel. It'd take us, like, a year.'

'That sort of thing only works in stories,' Gil said. 'We could use Junk as a watch dog,' he added. 'To raise the alarm if anyone comes near, but he doesn't bark, does he? I don't think I've *ever* heard him bark.'

'He's too smart to bark,' Riley said. 'If anyone tries to attack us, Junk won't waste time barking. He'll leap straight for their throat. Isn't that right, Junk?'

Junk blinked amiably and thumped his tail against the ground. 'What about this for an idea?' Riley said. 'We take the petrol out of the car and pour it in a big circle around the camp, and the minute the man comes close, we light it and...' Riley flung out his arms. '*WHOOOOOSH!*'

The others stared at him silently.

'Okay, I guess that's not such a great idea,' Riley muttered.

In the end, they decided to keep their preparations simple. For a couple of days – three, to be on the safe side – they would do without a fire in case the area was being watched. In addition, they would keep noise to a minimum and stay well away from the perimeter of the island to avoid being spotted from the road.

Everyone agreed that if the man came, he would wait until night, when there wasn't much chance of drawing attention to himself. They would have to keep watch, taking it in turns to stay awake.

'How will we know when it's the next person's turn?' Riley wanted to know. 'We don't have a way of telling time and it'll be dark.'

Nobody had an answer to this. They could have used the stars, or the moon only they didn't know how, and even if they did it wouldn't be much help if the night was cloudy.

It was Pez who finally came up with a solution. She fetched a mug and mimed drinking. Then she put the mug down and stared at her wrist, as if reading a watch.

'I don't get it,' Grayson said.

Pez looked embarrassed. She mimed drinking again, stood up and disappeared behind a nearby tree.

'Still don't get it,' Riley said.

'I do!' Gil cried. 'What she's trying to say is that you drink some water, and after a while – a couple of hours or so – you need to pee. It's a way of telling time – not very accurate, maybe, but good enough for when we're keeping watch. We drink a mug of water at the start of our turn, and by the time we need to pee, it's the next person's turn.'

'Genius,' Riley whispered, after a stupefied pause. 'Sheer *genius*...'

After that was settled, the boys turned to the question of weapons. If the worst came to the worst, they needed to be able to defend themselves. Pez had her slingshot. She also had a small axe that she used for chopping branches, but none of the boys – not even Riley – liked the idea of carrying it around, let alone using it as a weapon.

In the end, they decided to make use of the golf clubs that Riley had stolen shortly before Gil arrived on the island. Riley fetched the golf bag and distributed the clubs, and they spent a while swinging them – sending tufts of earth flying in every direction – before making their choice.

They had a plan, they had weapons. All they had to do now was wait and watch.

The next three days passed with agonising slowness, each hour longer than the one before. Without a fire, there was no coffee in the morning and nothing to gather around when evening fell. The boys worked on the construction of Junk's tepee and invented a way of playing golf using peach stones for balls, but mostly they rested, trying to make up for lost sleep.

Supper – when it came – was a dismal affair, the food eaten cold from the last of the tins that Riley and Grayson had brought with them. They were the last of the tins for a reason, as Gil soon discovered.

'Kidney beans?' he said. 'What made you buy *kidney beans*?'

'We were in a hurry,' Riley said. 'We weren't looking at the labels.'

'Try eating them with a bit of tomato paste,' Grayson said, handing him another tin. 'Makes them taste different.'

'Not better,' he added sadly. 'Just different...'

Although the days dragged, the nights were even worse. Gil dreaded the moment when it was his turn to keep watch. It wasn't so much the boredom – although that was bad enough – it was the way that everything took on a different shape in the dark. He sat on his tin stool, his golf club held tight across his knees, and saw lurking figures in every shadow, monsters among the branches of every tree.

In the light of day, it was relatively easy to distract himself. But alone at night – no matter how hard he tried – his mind would return to the dark-haired man's face. And each time it did, the face grew bigger and the flesh more deeply lined, until it no longer looked human. Not the face of a man, but the leering mask of a gargoyle, grotesque and pitiless.

He won't come, Gil told himself. *He won't. But if he does, we're ready.*

Thirty-nine

On the third night of the vigil, Gil dreamed about his parents again. The dream started the same way the first one had. He was standing on the beach, watching his parents paddle away, shouting as loudly as he could, although no sound came out. Any minute now, he would see Ms Lundy, Gil thought in the dream. He turned to look.

It wasn't Ms Lundy. It was the orange teddy bear from Gil's first foster home. He was much bigger than Gil remembered, almost as tall as he was, and his eyes – always huge – were now the size of saucepan lids.

Why did you throw me away? the bear said in a jarring, high-pitched voice. *Wasn't I good enough? You never gave me a chance...*

Gil's parents were now much further away, mere dots against the blue.

It's all your fault! the bear suddenly shrieked. *You're the one to blame!*

'That's not true!' Gil yelled, but it was too late. He was already awake. Grayson was shaking his arm, telling him it was his turn to stand guard.

It was the last watch of the night. Dawn was not far away. The darkness was thinning into grey. Gil sat in his usual spot, his arms wrapped around his chest, waiting for the terrible image of the orange teddy bear to fade from his mind.

It was the anniversary of his parents' death, although he was the only person who knew that fact. For everyone else in the world, it was simply another day. *It's not the sort of thing to share*, Gil thought. It wasn't like a birthday, or a special holiday, something to celebrate with others. It was the opposite of that – a feeling of being utterly alone.

He fetched the photo of his parents from his back pocket. After the storm, he had dried and smoothed it out as best he could, yet there wasn't much left of it. His mum's hand was still there and the collar of his dad's shirt, and part of the railing they were leaning against. But where the rest had been – Niagara Falls in the background, his parents' smiling faces – there was nothing now but empty space.

A great loneliness filled Gil's heart. It was the deepest kind of loneliness, the kind that feels worse instead of better when people are around, however friendly they may be. He glanced over at the tepees. Riley and Grayson would be awake soon, Pez too. They would be in a hurry to get up, eager for a hot cup of coffee. After three days, even Grayson had agreed that they could go back to having a fire. They would continue to keep watch for a couple more nights, but the danger was past. If the man had been looking, he would either have found them by now, or given up and gone away.

Gil didn't want to face them just yet. He got up, and without thinking what he was doing, acting only on impulse, began making his way towards the far end of the island, away from Pez's camp and beyond the bathroom hole, to where the trees grew particularly thick.

It was a part of the island they didn't often visit. Gil had been once or twice, but the undergrowth was too dense to get through easily, and there was little food around, so there had never been much reason to linger there.

Thorns tore at his jeans as he pushed through the bushes, using his golf club to help clear a path. The trees grew so close that he had to crouch to get past fallen branches, stumbling over roots at almost every step. He turned sideways, squeezed through a gap between two tree trunks, and stopped.

He was in a clearing. A tree had fallen there, opening a small window to the sky, and nothing so far had grown to fill the gap. Gil found a perch on what was left of the trunk and sat for a long time, his mind empty of thought, his gaze fixed on a shadow at the base of a nearby tree.

The sky was light by the time he finally lifted his eyes, the clamour of birdsong already filling the air.

The sun would be up soon. He ought to be getting back; Riley and Grayson must be wondering where he was. But they felt strangely distant, as distant as the birds and the motorway traffic, and Gil made no effort to stir. Even the beating of his heart seemed far away. Without thinking, he lifted the hagstone to his eye.

The shadow he'd been looking at wasn't a shadow. He could see that now. It was a hole, dug in the shelter between two roots, its mouth no wider than Gil's fist. Brightness flickered through the trees and a ray of light – the first of the day – fell across the area of ground in front of the hole. In the same instant – as if the sun itself had summoned it into existence – Gil saw the fox.

He was heading towards the hole, trotting along in the high stepping way of all foxes, lean and light-footed. There was something held in his jaws, although it was a second before Gil realised what it was. Then he saw it was a cricket.

It hunts insects, he thought. *The same way a regular fox hunts rabbits...*

The fox reached the hole and darted inside with a whisk of its brushy tail. Gil stared after it, frozen by amazement, hardly daring to breathe. A breeze stirred the leaves of the topmost trees, and the contrail of a plane slowly stitched the patch of sky above his head. The ray of sun at the mouth of the fox's hole widened and spread.

Then, as swiftly as he had vanished, the fox emerged again, only this time he wasn't alone. As he slipped out of his lair, there was a second fox behind him, closely followed by three cubs. Gil's heart almost burst with delight.

If the adults were the size of cats, the fox cubs were no larger than kittens, their fur glowing orange in the sunlight as they played together.

It's a whole family, Gil thought. But where had they come from? Was it possible they were an entirely new species? Gil wondered how many other animals there were, living in the places that humans overlooked. Animals that had changed and adapted, unnoticed by the world. All of them at home on Nowhere Island.

He must have shifted slightly, or perhaps it was a passing shadow – a hawk or owl – that raised the alarm. In a flash, the foxes were gone.

Gil let out a long breath, blinking as if waking from a trance. There was no point staying where he was. It might be hours before the foxes came out again. In a little while, he would leap to his feet. He would race back to the camp and tell the others what he'd seen. And this time, it wouldn't be a story he was making up, it would be for *real*.

Not yet though. Not for a minute or two.

It was the anniversary of his parents' death. That was the reason he was there. If it hadn't been for his parents, he wouldn't have been in that place, alone with his thoughts, sitting so still that the foxes came out of their lair, yawning in the sunlight, their cubs tumbling around them.

His parents had gone. Even their faces had vanished from his photo. But they hadn't left. Gil saw that now.

They hadn't left because they were a part of everything he did, everything he thought. Because he carried them with him.

Not only today, but every day, for as long as he lived.

The sun was warm on the back of his neck. It was another glorious morning. Gil jumped up, and with a last look at the fox's hole, began making his way back through the dense undergrowth. He reached the meadow and saw a thin thread of smoke rising above the grass. They had lit the fire, the water in the pan already boiling, perhaps. And because it was a celebration – the first hot drink in three days – Grayson would let them have a spoon of sugar for their coffee.

Gil began to run. Riley and Grayson were sitting by the fire as he rushed up, his voice bubbling with excitement.

'You'll never guess what I saw,' he cried. 'A family! A whole family of—'

He broke off. They weren't looking at him. Gil turned his head to see what they were staring at.

The man was on the island. He was walking straight towards them.

Forty

The instant he saw him, Gil knew that everything they had done to prepare for this moment had been utterly useless. It wasn't just the man's height, or the broad stretch of his shoulders. It was the deliberate, unhurried way he was walking, as if setting about some ordinary, routine chore, that made any attempt to fight him seem completely impossible.

Riley and Grayson must have realised it too, for neither of them moved. They simply stood in helpless silence as the man approached. Gil suddenly saw what should have been obvious all along. They weren't pirates or outlaws or cunning desperadoes, armed and ready for any attack. They were kids. Three frightened, grubby-looking boys.

The man stopped an arm's length away and stared at them for a moment. There was something strange about his gaze. As if he was looking through them, rather than at them. As if they were merely obstacles, standing in his line of sight.

The man's eyes fell on the golf club, hanging limply from Grayson's hand.

'Having a game?' he said. 'What are you using for balls?'

'Peach stones,' Grayson muttered.

The man didn't smile or even change expression. He nodded.

'Drop it,' he said. 'You too,' he added, glancing at Gil's club.

'Build up the fire,' the man said, after they'd let go of the clubs. 'I got cold, waiting for the sun to rise.'

Riley fetched wood from the pile, and silently placed it on the fire. Gil's dread deepened. Even Riley was doing what he was told. Nobody had asked the man who he was, or what he was doing there, and it wasn't because they already knew. It was because *he* knew they knew, and it was pointless to pretend otherwise.

This isn't a game, Gil thought. *And everyone knows it.*

He wondered if Pez had seen the man arrive. She must have done. Was she watching them right now, coming up with a plan...?

The man sat on one of the tin stools and spread his hands over the fire to warm them. He was wearing a nylon jacket and black dress pants, neatly pressed, although there were traces of mud on the knees. He brought a handkerchief out of his jacket pocket and began wiping the dirt off his shoes, almost fussily, his mouth twisted with distaste.

'How did you know we were here?' Riley said.

'I remembered the dog,' the man said, without looking up from his task. 'From a couple of weeks ago.'

The night they stole the cake, Gil thought. Junk had trotted into the rest stop before they could prevent him. They should have paid attention to that. They'd been so careful to stay hidden and keep on the island, but they'd forgotten that Junk came and went as he pleased.

'He looked like he belonged to someone,' the man said, still buffing his shoes. 'I thought he'd likely come back. All I had to do was wait.'

'You followed him here?'

As if he knew he was being talked about, Junk suddenly appeared from behind a tepee. The man fetched a scrap from his pocket and tossed it into the dog's open mouth. 'That's the ugliest mutt I've ever seen,' he said.

Junk grinned and went into his begging position. The man threw him another scrap.

'Junk! How could you?' Riley said in anguish.

'It's not his fault,' Grayson said. 'He didn't mean to get us into trouble.'

'I know,' Riley said sadly. 'He can't help it. He'll do anything for food…'

The man had returned to his shoes, apparently bored by the conversation. Gil wondered if he'd even been listening. He had the feeling that the man only paid attention to what he needed to. Everything else was background noise. He finished wiping, folded the handkerchief into a square and replaced it in his pocket. Then he turned his gaze back to the boys.

Gil saw his eyes weren't particularly dark. They just looked that way because there was no light inside them, not the smallest spark.

'So, where's your friend?' the man said.

Gil's heart thudded. Pez mustn't be found. She was their only hope.

'What friend?' he said, a little too quickly.

'There's only three of us,' Riley said. 'That's it.'

'So why are there four stools around your fire?'

Nobody answered. Gil tried to think of something to say, but his mind had gone completely blank.

'We use the other one to put stuff on,' Riley said at last. 'Like a table…'

The man raised his hand, and without taking his eyes off Riley, began stroking Junk's head.

'I like dogs,' he said. 'I'd hate to have to hurt one.'

The words had come out so casually, Gil thought for a second that he must have misheard. He glanced at the others in horror. But neither Riley nor Grayson seemed shocked. They simply looked resigned.

They're used to being threatened, Gil thought. *It doesn't surprise them. Their dad made sure of that.*

They had escaped their home, survived for weeks by themselves, and proved their courage again and again. Yet none of that seemed to matter now. In less than a minute, the brothers had gone back to the small, bullied kids they used to be. It was as if the man had shrunk them. For the first time that morning, Gil felt the rise of anger.

'Leave Junk alone!' he cried. 'There *is* someone else. I'll go get her if you like.'

'Where is she?'

'She might be in those trees,' Gil said with a vague sweep of his arm, 'or maybe by the pond...'

The man looked at him. 'I know what you're thinking,' he said. 'You're thinking you'll get halfway to the trees and then you'll make a dash for the road. Try to flag down a car.'

'No, I wasn't,' Gil protested, although it was exactly what'd he'd been thinking. That getting to the motorway was their only chance. The cars might be moving fast, but someone would see him. Someone would stop.

'Not a good idea,' the man said, still stroking Junk's head. 'It's dangerous to run into traffic, you know. But let's say you get someone to stop. You'll tell them to call the police, right?' The man paused, staring at Gil. He had spoken softly, almost playfully. But there was nothing playful in his dark, unblinking gaze.

'We're in the middle of nowhere,' the man said. 'Any idea how long it will take the police to get here? I'm guessing it will be a while. By that time, it will be too late. And not just for your dog.' The man rose to his feet, and before Gil knew what he was doing, he was standing behind Riley, his hands resting on the boy's trembling shoulders.

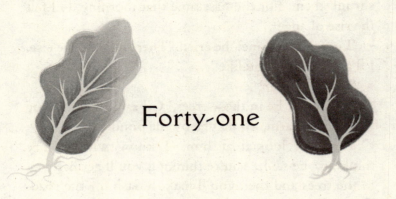

Forty-one

'Here's what you're going to do,' the man told Gil. 'You're going to walk over to the trees, nice and slow, keeping your hands where I can see them. Before you get there, you're going to stop and call for your friend to come out.'

'What if she doesn't?'

'Then you've got a problem,' the man said.

Gil glanced at the others, but they were staring at the ground, their heads held low.

'Off you go,' the man said.

It seemed to take an eternity to cross the meadow. As if the world had slowed to give Gil time to notice every detail. The dryness of his throat, the light on the grass, the warm, sweet smell of clover, each separate trill and whistle of the birds. The sound of traffic had been growing steadily during the last hour, but it didn't change anything, he thought. Nobody knew they were there or could see what was happening.

Their invisibility had always kept them safe. Now it was the reason they were in such danger. It was as if the island itself had turned against them.

He was almost at the trees. He knew he was being watched, but Gil forced himself not to turn and look, because it would make him seem frightened, and he refused to give the man that satisfaction.

Pez had emerged from the shadows and was already walking towards him, looking scared, yet utterly resolute. Her slingshot was tucked into her belt behind her back, and as she approached, she uncurled her fist and Gil saw a single pebble lying in the palm of her hand.

'It'll be okay,' he said softly. 'We'll think of something. I know we will.'

Riley had added more wood to the fire. It was crackling fiercely now, flames licking the air. They never allowed the fire to get this big in the daytime. Riley must have done it on purpose, in the hope of attracting attention. If so, it was a desperate hope, as thin as the smoke itself, dispersing in the breeze.

The man glanced at Pez without expression as they joined the others.

'You can sit down,' he said. 'The big guy near me, where I can keep an eye on him. You're not going to cause any trouble, are you, big guy?'

Grayson shook his head meekly, shoulders hunched.

'Okay,' the man said. 'Here's the thing. You took something that belongs to me. All you have to do is give it back and then I'm gone. You can carry on – '

his gaze settled for a second on Riley's pirate flag –
'playing your games.'

He was lying, Gil knew it. It wasn't just the blank
indifference in the man's eyes, or the way he spoke so
casually about hurting them. It was his lack of curiosity
that frightened Gil the most. The man hadn't asked
them what they were doing on the island, how they
had got there or where they had come from. He hadn't
even asked their names. They meant nothing to him, Gil
thought. They were simply obstacles in his line of sight.

'Give it back and I'm gone,' the man repeated.

'If we do that, you'll leave us alone?' Riley said.
'You promise?'

Gil stared at Riley. Surely, he knew the man was
lying. Why hadn't Riley denied having the bag of
money? The man might not have believed him, but it
would have bought some time at least. It might have
given them a chance to escape.

'So, where's my bag?' the man said.

Gil was certain Riley would tell him he'd hung it
from the tallest branch in the lookout tree. Or buried
it in the middle of the meadow. Or taken the bundles
of cash and hidden them in fifty different places.
Anything to distract the man and send him on a wild
goose chase.

'It's in my tepee,' Riley said.

'Then you'd better go and fetch it.'

'Don't do it!' Gil cried.

Riley didn't respond, or even look at him. He went
over to his tepee and disappeared inside, and for half

a second, Gil felt a shred of hope. Riley must have something up his sleeve. He *must.*

But when Riley came out of his tepee, the only thing he had was the bag. He brought it over and placed it on the ground without saying anything.

'That's a good boy,' the man said.

There was such a look of defeat on Riley's face that Gil wanted to cry.

'Unzip it,' the man said.

Riley did as he was told, his hands shaking. He spread the bag open to show the money, then slowly zipped it up again.

'Bring it here,' the man said.

Riley hesitated. 'You'll let us go? You promised, right?'

'I said so, didn't I?'

'Okay,' Riley said. 'Okay…' He reached for the bag, his fingers tightening around the handles. But just before he did so, he glanced at Grayson and Gil saw something flash between them for a split-second. A kind of electricity.

Nobody can read minds, Gil thought with a wild thump of his heart. *It's impossible…*

Riley seized the bag. 'Catch!' he cried, and hurled it into the fire.

Three things happened in lightning-fast succession. The fire, already large, gave a great *whoosh* as the bag – and the paper inside – burst into flame. The man lunged, trying to grab it, and in the same instant, Grayson swung back his arm.

The whole of his life was in that arm. Every punch he hadn't given. Every moment he had stopped himself from hitting back. Grayson had never struck anyone before, but he must have thought of it a thousand times, for his aim was perfect. Gil heard the crack of fist meeting jaw, and the thud as the man fell.

'Get him!' Riley screamed.

Forty-two

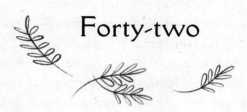

All four of them were on him in an instant, Grayson's knee in his back, Pez using her belt to tie his feet.

'We need something for his hands,' Riley panted, tearing off his green silk bandana. 'Hold him still!'

The man made no sound as they struggled to subdue him. He lay still, every muscle in his body tense.

'Can he move?' Riley asked.

'I don't think so,' Grayson said, tugging on the knots.

They backed away, keeping a wary distance. Then, as if suddenly remembering its existence, they all turned to look at the fire. There was nothing left of the bag and its contents but a charred scrap of nylon and a pile of ashes.

'You were planning it all along,' Gil said to Riley. 'That's why you built up the fire.'

'I don't know,' Riley said, his voice shaky. 'I guess so, but if it wasn't for Gray…'

Grayson stared down at his fist as if seeing it for the first time, his face troubled.

'What do we do now?' Gil said. 'We can't keep him tied up for ever…'

'And we can't let him go,' Riley added.

'Do you think he was going to kill us?' Gil said.

'Maybe,' Grayson said. 'We don't know that for sure, and even if he was, it doesn't make any difference.'

'I guess there's only one thing we *can* do,' Gil said.

Grayson nodded. 'If we build a ramp behind the car, it'll be easier to push on to the road. We can use the branches from our tepees. We'll be seen, of course, but it won't matter if we make a quick getaway.'

Now that the decision had been made, Gil felt an unexpected lightening of his heart. *We're running away again*, he thought. *All of us together. The island was our home, but there are other islands to find. The world is full of secret places. All we have to do is look.*

While Grayson stayed by the fire, keeping guard over the man, the others hurried to dismantle the tepees, carrying the branches between them, and arranging them as best they could to form a slope for the car.

There was nothing left to do but pack their few belongings and put out the fire for the last time.

'What are we going to do about *him*?' Gil asked. The man had made no move to escape while Grayson had been watching him, nor had he spoken. And when Grayson held a cup of water to his lips, he had turned his head away.

'He's waiting for us to go,' Grayson said. 'He's only tied with a belt and a bit of cloth. It might take him a while, but he'll free himself sooner or later.'

'Where's Pez?' Gil said suddenly.

He could have sworn she'd been with them a moment ago. Now she was nowhere to be seen.

Forty-three

Pez was crouched by her vegetable patch, loosening the soil with her trowel. It didn't need to be loosened, but she couldn't think of anything else to do to stop herself from crying. The bird stood nearby, waiting for any worms she might find, his eyes fixed on the turning soil.

She saw the boys approaching through the trees, and abruptly bent her head. She knew they'd come looking for her, although part of her wished they hadn't bothered. It would have been easier if they'd gone away without saying anything. It would have got it over with, at least.

'What are you doing?' Gil said. 'Why aren't you packing? We're leaving in a few minutes.'

Pez carried on as if she hadn't heard, although she wasn't loosening the soil any longer, she was just stabbing the ground with her trowel.

'You can't stay here,' Grayson said. 'It's not safe.'

'I don't get it,' Riley said. 'You could've stayed hidden when that man sent Gil to look for you, but you didn't. I thought you were on our side. We're a team, aren't we?'

'We're more than a team,' Gil burst out. 'We're a family.' He glanced at the others, as if expecting them to laugh, but their faces were solemn.

Pez couldn't see what she was doing, her eyes had filled with tears.

'Most of my life I've been waiting for a family to choose me,' Gil said. 'And it never happened. I used to think it was because I wasn't good enough, and maybe I wasn't, but that shouldn't have mattered.'

Pez wanted to wipe her face, but her hands were covered with mud, and it would have made no difference anyway. Her tears were falling much too fast.

'It shouldn't have mattered because it's not about being good enough,' Gil said, his words coming out in a rush. 'It isn't about fitting in or whether it's convenient or not, or even where you're born. It's where you *belong*, Pez. That's what a family is.'

There was a helpless look on his face, as if he knew that no matter how hard he tried, he would never find the right words. That what he felt was too big and too important to ever properly explain.

'He's right!' Riley exclaimed. 'I never thought of it like that before, but he's right.'

'Not where you're born,' Grayson echoed. 'Where you belong…'

'And you belong with us,' Riley said.

'Don't you *want* to come?' Gil's voice was desperate.

Pez couldn't bring herself to shake her head.

'Then why are you staying?' Gil cried.

Pez couldn't tell him because she couldn't speak. But even if she could, he would never understand.

'It's the condor, isn't it?' Grayson said suddenly. 'You don't want to leave him behind.'

Pez nodded, too miserable to try to deny it. She didn't know why the bird had stayed with her so long. It wasn't simply because she'd kept feeding him. He could have found food for himself – much more than she'd been able to provide – if he'd taken to the air. Perhaps he had a hidden injury that prevented him from flying, despite his healthy appearance. Or maybe he hadn't flown for so long that he'd forgotten how to. Whatever the reason, Pez couldn't abandon him now. He would starve. He needed her.

'We can't take him with us,' Gil said. 'He wouldn't fit in the car.'

'Well, he might,' Grayson said, 'although there wouldn't be much room for anyone else.'

Pez didn't want to listen. She was all the bird had. He needed her.

Or is it me who needs him? Pez thought.

'Junk wouldn't like having him in the car,' Riley said. 'They'd spend the whole time arguing in the back seat. It'd drive us crazy.'

Pez smiled despite herself. It was watery and unwilling, but it was still a smile.

'He doesn't belong here,' Gil told her gently. 'He has to go home.'

Pez hesitated then stood up and wiped her eyes with her sleeve. They were right. And she was no better than the Starborn if she ignored the truth. The bird's huge wingspan was evidence that he wasn't made for life among the trees. He needed space and height, mountains and canyons, thermals of air to ride, along with the great storm clouds.

He had to go home.

Pez knew the bird was too big and heavy to take off among the trees. He needed room to gain momentum. She shooed him gently to the edge of the meadow.

The bird was not used to being shooed. It startled him into a lurching, undignified trot, and there was a reproachful look in his eye when he finally came to a stop. The three boys and Pez stood staring at him, not sure what to do next.

Gil clapped his hands. 'Time to go. You can do it!'

The bird looked away and began preening his ruffled feathers in an exaggerated fashion, as if emphasising how badly he'd been treated.

'Get going, Baldy,' Riley cried. 'You big old lump!'

'He won't do it if you're rude,' Grayson said.

'He doesn't know I'm being rude. I could be saying anything for all he knows. And he *is* bald, so that's not—'

'I've got an idea,' Gil interrupted. 'Grayson said he wouldn't fly away because he was waiting for something. Do you remember? And then, after the storm, he only came out of hiding when Riley told him to come out. I think that's what he's waiting for. To be told to leave.'

'We *are* telling him!'

'Not us,' Gil said. 'Pez has to do it.'

Everyone was suddenly looking at her. 'That's it,' Riley said. 'It's got to be.'

Pez shook her head. It wasn't true. She had told the bird to leave a hundred times in her mind.

'He has to *hear* it,' Grayson said. 'You have to tell him out loud.'

'We won't listen,' Riley said. 'We'll cover our ears. You can yell at the top of your voice, and we won't hear a thing.'

Pez gazed at the three boys, their hands squeezed tight against their ears. Riley and Grayson were staring at the ground. Only Gil was looking at her, his eyes filled with encouragement.

Pez turned to the bird. Was it true? Would he leave if she spoke?

'*Please,*' she whispered but her throat was too full of cobwebs to make a sound, and she was suddenly terrified that she had left it too late. She had forgotten how to speak and would have to spend the rest of her life in silence, reaching for words that never came. *But I have so much to say*, Pez thought in desperation.

She pressed her hand against her heart, holding it safe.

'*Please*,' she said, and her voice sounded strange in her ears, high and clear, like the voice of someone else. Someone who had once loved to talk and sing and ask a thousand questions.

'Go home,' Pez said.

The bird swivelled his head and looked at her with surprise. The boys had taken their hands away from their ears and were gaping at her too, but Pez barely noticed.

'You don't have to look after me any more,' Pez told the bird.

The condor took a few shuffling steps forward and stopped.

'You're scared you've forgotten how to do it,' Pez said. 'I was scared too, but I haven't forgotten and nor have you.'

Perhaps the bird really *could* understand her, for he immediately broke into a run, his wings flailing as if he wasn't entirely sure how they worked or what to do with them.

'I love you,' Pez whispered.

His wings were raised now, reaching. Then they unfolded and Pez caught her breath at the vastness of their span, their shadow stretching from one edge of the meadow to the other. The wings gave a great beat, and then another, and with the third –

'Yay! Yay!' the boys cheered, jumping, and flinging out their arms.

Pez kept her gaze on the condor. He cleared the trees and dipped out of sight for a second. Then he was rising once more. He was a different creature now, all his awkwardness gone, his wings barely shifting as he climbed the blue ladder of the sky. Up and up he went until he was no more than a speck against the sun. Then he was gone.

Pez turned. The others were staring at her as though she had sprouted wings herself.

'Hi,' she said, suddenly feeling shy. But they seemed just as tongue-tied.

'You can't just talk,' Riley spluttered at last. 'You can talk to *animals*…'

'Fact,' Grayson murmured.

'We don't even know your name,' Gil said, his face going red.

She hesitated. Her parents had given her a name, yet she didn't have to keep it. She could be anyone she wanted to be.

'It's Pez,' she said, smiling at him.

Forty-four

'So, where are we going to go?' Pez asked as they made their way to the boys' camp.

Gil frowned. 'Not back to Ms Lundy, that's for sure.'

'And not back to our dad,' Riley said. 'We'd rather eat crickets for the rest of our lives, wouldn't we, Gray?'

'What about that lady?' Grayson asked. 'The one who lived near the beach.'

'Helen?' Gil shook his head. 'Even if she wanted to look after us, she wouldn't be allowed. I don't see why we have to go back to anyone. Why can't we stay on our own?'

'Easier said than done,' Riley said.

'Think about it!' Gil said, his voice rising with excitement. 'We don't need anyone to look after us, we've proved that we can look after ourselves. And we don't need to find a family because we're *already* a family. We don't even need to go to school. We can teach each other. Grayson can teach us how to fix stuff and drive a car and whittle wood…'

'That's true, I could,' Grayson said.

'And Pez can teach us about nature and science, and I can teach how to tell stories and all the best books to read. I bet we'd learn way more than we would in an ordinary, boring school.'

'Hang on a minute,' Riley said. 'You didn't say what *I'm* going to teach. It's not fair if I don't get to teach!'

Gil caught Grayson's eye, and quickly suppressed a smile.

'I'm sure we'll think of something,' he said.

The man was still lying where they'd left him, although it was clear he'd been busy while they'd been away, for the scarf around his wrists was torn, as if he'd been trying to undo it with his teeth.

'We should get going,' Grayson said. 'Those knots won't hold him for much longer.

'But we don't have to make it easy for him, do we?' Riley said. He crouched beside the man, searching through his pockets.

'What are you looking for?' Gil asked.

'These!' Riley cried, flourishing a set of car keys. 'I'm going to throw 'em down the bathroom hole.'

'That hole is kind of full,' he told the man. 'You're

going to have to fish if you want your keys back. That's what you get for calling Junk an ugly mutt, when he's not ugly *or* a mutt. For your information, he's a pure-bred Saharan hunting dog.' Riley paused for a second, savouring his triumph.

'So put *that* in your pipe and smoke it,' he said.

With the four of them pushing, it only took a few moments to roll the car out of the trees and on to the grass verge of the motorway.

'Shotgun!' Riley cried, making a dive for the front seat. Junk was already in the back, thumping his tail and grinning.

'You sure you can drive?' Gil said as Grayson started the engine.

'He got us here, didn't he?' Riley snapped.

The car shot backwards. 'Sorry, didn't mean to do that,' Grayson mumbled, fumbling with the gears.

'Stop yanking the wheel like that,' Riley said. 'You'll pull it right off!'

'You've still got the handbrake on!' Gil cried.

'Put it in first!' Riley yelped

Pez tapped Grayson on the shoulder. 'You've got this,' she said quietly. 'Just breathe, okay?'

'I've got this,' Grayson muttered, taking his foot off the brake, and easing the car around. 'I've got this...'

'Wait for an opening,' Pez told him. 'After that yellow truck...'

Grayson pressed his foot on the accelerator and the car swung on to the motorway.

'Open your eyes!' Riley shrieked.

'I only closed them for a second,' Grayson protested.

They picked up speed and Gil gazed at the island flashing past. They were on the other side of it now. He was seeing it as a passer-by. Nothing more than a blur of trees, indistinguishable from all the other green spaces scattered along the motorway.

'Do you think we'd ever be able to find it again?' he said.

Nobody answered. There was a troubled look on Grayson's face.

'I thought we had more petrol than that,' he said, his eyes flickering towards the dashboard.

'Maybe it's busted,' Riley said, tapping the fuel gauge.

Gil's heart sank so suddenly that he almost groaned out loud. What a fool he'd been. Thinking they could stay together and look after themselves. It was just another one of his stupid stories, and not even a particularly good one, because he'd forgotten the most basic thing of all.

'We don't have any money,' he said. 'All I've got is nineteen dollars and fifty cents. That's not even enough to halfway fill the tank.'

They would have to go back to where they came from after all. And it would be even worse than before because of the trouble they'd caused. They'd probably be watched the whole time, and they'd certainly never see each other again. Not until they were grown up, and by that time they'd have forgotten all about the summer they spent on an island in the middle of nowhere.

The summer they became a family.

'Pity all that cash burned,' Riley said, his voice airy. 'Complete waste of fifty thousand dollars.'

Grayson looked confused. 'Don't you mean two hundred and fifty? I counted it myself.'

'You think I'd throw a quarter million dollars on the fire?' Riley's voice rose in outrage. 'It was bad enough burning fifty thousand! But I had to. I filled the bag with leaves and stuff and put the cash on top.'

'Leaves?' Grayson said, still struggling to understand.

'And a pair of your smelly socks,' Riley said. 'The rest of the money is in the bag with the golf clubs. And there's no point saying we have to give it back, Gray, because we can't. Even you've got to admit that.'

Grayson shook his head. 'You're *bad*, Riley...'

'Somebody has to be,' Riley said. 'You were dead wrong about me not having anything to teach. I have *loads*.'

'Two hundred thousand dollars,' Pez whispered. 'That's a lot, right?'

'We're rich,' Gil marvelled. 'We can do what we want. Go where we want. We can find a new place to live. Somewhere *great*.'

He gazed at the motorway stretching ahead. Sooner or later, they would come to a sign for a turning they might take, one road leading to the mountains, another to the sea, a third winding by fields and barns and covered bridges over streams. It didn't matter where they went, so long as they kept going in the right direction.

Gil reached for the hagstone around his neck. What had Helen told him he'd see when he looked through the hole?

A different world, perhaps a better one.

'We just have to keep looking,' Gil said.

Enjoy reading

The Time Traveller and the TIGER

Out now in paperback

One

1946. CENTRAL INDIA.

*I*t was so still, John was sure it was dead.

He didn't know how long he'd been standing there, rigid with shock and disbelief. The birds had risen shrieking from the trees and answering cries of alarm had filled the forest. Now a hush had fallen over the clearing. John stepped forward, still holding the gun in both hands, his eyes locked on the body in the grass. It lay with its back to him, its colour even more improbable in the hard, open glare of the midday sun. He took a few more steps and stopped, his heart thudding. Insects pulsed steadily in the undergrowth and an invisible woodpecker tapped, paused, and tapped again.

John leaned closer, craning his neck.

The tiger snarled and twisted with shocking ferocity, striking too fast for John to see. He felt his feet leave the ground; a confusion of sky, muscled fur and burning breath. Then pain tore through his body, and the world went out.

It was dark when he opened his eyes. He was half on his back, half on his side. There were stars in the sky, and in the corner of his vision, the black shapes of trees. His gun lay nearby, moonlight glinting on the barrel, although he couldn't reach it. Something hot and vastly heavy was preventing him from moving his legs. He raised his head.

His heart staggered and seemed to stop.

The tiger was lying on top of him, pinning him from the waist down. John could smell the sharp, musky, overpowering scent of its skin, could see the slope of its back, ten shades darker than the night sky. As he stared, the slope rose a fraction and he felt a shudder run through the tiger's body.

It was still alive!

Every atom in John's body froze. Then his heart bounded into frenzy, and the stars above him trembled, as if the sky itself was being shaken. Any second now, the tiger would turn and kill him. John wished he was already dead, just to have it over and done with, just to stop the awful pounding in his chest. With a great effort, he managed to raise his right hand. He clutched the front of his shirt and waited.

Nothing moved. Only the cold night breeze in the grass, and the slope of the tiger's back as it breathed.

No tiger lay out in the open, especially one that was wounded. John didn't need Mandeep to tell him that.

It would drag itself to cover if it could. He felt another breath fill the tiger's body and pass slowly away.

The animal was too hurt to seek refuge. It couldn't move, any more than he could. They were in the same boat, the tiger and him. For a second, John had an image of a fishing vessel with narrow hull and snug canopy, the tiger steering with a long oar at the stern, while John kept watch at the bow. The image was so clear and so bizarre, he felt a spark of hope. Perhaps he was dreaming. Fast asleep under a mosquito net in his bedroom at home. Safe.

Then the pain came back. It came suddenly, as if – like the tiger – it had been waiting to strike, spreading from his right leg in a knife-sharpened wave. He heard himself groan, and as if in answer, the distant *whoop-whoop* of langur monkeys. The sky blurred.

Time passed. He couldn't tell if it was a minute or an hour. He found the pain was slightly less if he twisted his shoulder to one side. He grabbed a clump of grass to hold himself in place and clenched his teeth.

His leg must be broken, he thought. It was a miracle he wasn't dead. The tiger could have killed him easily. Mandeep said…

His head swam, his hold on the grass slippery with sweat.

Mandeep said that a tiger's forepaw was powerful enough to knock a full-grown bull off its feet, and deft enough to catch a passing fly. Once, during a hunt, a tiger had sprung from the bushes and leaped over the head of one of the beaters. It had barely brushed the man as it passed. Yet when the others went to help the beater to his feet, they found him dead. The tiger had snapped his neck as if it were a twig.

If a tiger wants to kill you, Mandeep had once told John, there is no power on earth that can stop it.

It didn't want to kill me, John thought. *It was only defending itself.*

His mind wandered. Back at home they would have missed him by nightfall, although it would have been pointless to send a search party. They would be waiting for first light before setting out to look for him. By then it might be too late. John wondered how his parents would feel if he died. Sad, of course. But mostly disappointed at how badly he had let them down.

The pain had grown distant. In its place was a creeping chill, as if his bones were turning to ice.

He stared at the tiger's dark bulk. Its breath seemed slower than before, and he found himself counting each rise and fall.

One... two...

Perhaps if he tried, he could count them in to morning, he and the tiger, together in the same boat.

Eight... nine...

The boat had a blue canopy; water droplets flew, sparkling as the long oar dipped. All he had to do was concentrate, and he could count them in to shore, across the teeming, earth-brown river.

John had loosened his grip on the clump of grass some time ago. Now, barely knowing what he was doing, he lifted his hand and placed it on the tiger's back, palm flat against the warm, silky hide.

Thirty-seven… thirty…

The sky grew pearly and the low mist of dawn gathered above the tall grasses, turning their tips to silver. The sound of birds filled the air with a hundred different trills and babbles and whistling calls. But John was hardly aware of any of it. Somewhere, between one number and the next, he had hesitated. He had lost count. And now there was no point starting again.

The tiger lay still beneath his hand.

Far above, a vulture circled on broad, unhurried wings. John followed it with his eyes, feeling his mind drift from his body. He was with the vulture, looking down on himself. He saw his own face turned to the sky, saw the motionless body of the tiger. It looked far smaller than he remembered, already turning pale. The living flame of its skin fading to the colour of grass at the end of summer.

A terrible grief filled John's heart. A sense of wrongness that could never be put right. Tears rose in his eyes and ran unchecked down the side of his face. He heard a cry, the thump of running feet. The men in the search party were here. Mandeep was leaning over him, touching his hand.

John tried to speak but no words came.

'Be still,' Mandeep said.

He was carried home, one of the servants running ahead to fetch the doctor from town. His broken leg would never fully heal. He would always walk with a limp, although in time he would get used to it. In time, he would get used to many things. A new home, a new country, a different way of thinking about the world.

But all his life – even when he was an old man – he would carry the sense of wrongness he'd felt that morning when the tiger died. As if something had happened which wasn't meant to happen. As if a mistake had been made in the universe. And because of it, he would live his life the same way he walked.

Always just a little out of step.

ZEPHYR

We are an Empathy Builder Publisher

- Empathy is our ability to understand and share someone else's feelings
- It builds stronger, kinder communities
- It's a crucial life skill that can be learned

We are supporting **EmpathyLab** in their work to develop a book-based empathy movement in a drive to reach one million children a year and more.

Find out more at www.empathylab.uk
www.empathylab.uk/what-is-empathy-day

Zephyr is an imprint of Head of Zeus.
At Zephyr we are proud to publish books
you can read and re-read time and time
again because they tell a brilliant story
and because they entertain you.

@_ZephyrBooks

@_zephyrbooks

HeadofZeusBooks

readzephyr.com

www.headofzeus.com

ZEPHYR